Christmas Redemption

Three Girls' Journey

WELL OF LIFE
PUBLISHING

Christmas Redemption

Christmas Hotel Series Book Three

by

Saundra Staats McLemore

Christmas Redemption

Three Girls' Journey

Christmas Hotel Series Book Three

By Saundra Staats McLemore

Paperback ISBN: 978-0-9826750-8-3

Also available as an eBook
eBook ISBN: 978-0-9826750-7-6

First published by
Desert Breeze Publishing 2014
© Saundra Staats McLemore 2014

This new and revised edition
© Saundra Staats McLemore 2019

Content Editor: Chris Wright
Cover Artist: Gwen Phifer

Scripture Quotations are taken from the King James
Version of the Holy Bible

Published by

Well of Life Publishing
Ohio
United States of America

http://www.saundrastaatsmclemore.com

Other Books by Saundra Staats McLemore

The Staats Family Chronicles Series

Abraham and Anna – Book One of Staats Family Chronicles Series – Available now
Joy Out of Ashes
Book Two of Staats Family Chronicles Series
Available now

Christmas Hotel Series

Christmas Hotel (New edition)
Available now
Christmas for Lucy (New edition)
Available now
Christmas Redemption (New edition)
Available now
Christmas Pact (New edition)
Available October, 2019
Christmas Love and Mercy (New edition)
Available November, 2019
Christmas Hotel Reunion (New edition)
Available November, 2019

Dedication

I dedicate *Christmas Redemption* in the memory of Mary Callahan, Joyce Fullum, Kenneth Hazzard, and Susan Schreier. They were part of my sales and marketing staff at McLemore & Associates, Inc. They all left this earth in an untimely death. They are greatly missed by their "second family" at McLemore & Associates, Inc. All four believed in the message of *Christmas Redemption*.

Acknowledgements

I would like to thank Tony Staats for reading *Christmas Redemption* and helping to find all those typos!

I thank Franklin, Kentucky historian, Gayla McClary Coates, for the needed information regarding Franklin, Kentucky in 1967 for *Christmas Redemption*. She graciously answered my questions, and much of the information I was able to use for the accuracy of pertinent information in *Christmas Redemption*.

I would like to offer a special thank you to Sid and Jill Broderson for granting me permission to have my characters Christopher and Jerilyn Wright and their children, reside in their historical home at 210 South College Street in Franklin, Kentucky. This beautiful home is known in Franklin as the *Montague House* or the *Malone House*. The Italianate structure was built around 1860 by William Clement Montague.

Another special thank you to Barbara Beasley Smith and Jan Murphree for allowing me to have their fathers Dr. L. F. Beasley and Judge Joe Moss James "visit" the story.

As always, I thank my husband Robert E. McLemore for his complete support, as I enjoy the passion I have for writing.

I would like to thank our Lord and Savior Jesus Christ for the inspiration He provides for every story I write.

"For thou hast possessed my reins: thou hast covered me in my mother's womb.

I will praise thee; for I am fearfully and wonderfully made: marvelous are thy works; and that my soul knoweth right well.

My substance was not hid from thee, when I was made in secret, and curiously wrought in the lowest parts of the earth."

Psalms 139:13-15

Chapters

Chapter One

Cecilia

"And for this cause God shall send them strong delusion, that they should believe a lie."
2 Thessalonians 2:11

Houston, Texas
December 1, 1967
The cab driver turned in his seat and asked Cecilia if she was sure she wanted to go to the address she had given him. He had a kind face and his voice resonated concern, but his brow was furrowed with uncertainty. The name on his picture identification read Thomas Woodson.

Donna, a school friend, had given her the dubious address, and had merely said, "The doctor will take care of *it*." Cecilia said nothing, but nodded to the driver, and continued to look out the window. Mr. Woodson sped off to the other side of town; the seedy side of town. Although Cecilia entered the cab from Donna's apartment, she passed by the homes in her parents' middle class neighborhood, and then crossed the downtown business district.

They entered a rundown neighborhood to which she had never been. People stood and stared as her taxi drove past. Cecilia assumed taxis were a rare occurrence. She and her driver rode together in silence. From the corner of her eye she sensed him sometimes glancing back at her through the rearview mirror.

After a forty minute drive, Mr. Woodson stopped the car and turned to her again. "Miss, I just want to ask you one more time. Are you certain you want to be here? You can change your mind." His voice rang with so much concern that for a brief instant she considered taking his advice.

Cecilia gazed at the rundown building from the cab window. She looked down and checked the slip of paper, verifying the address. The address matched what was on the outside of the building. She turned back to the driver. In a thin voice she did not recognize as her own, she said, "I'm sure." The meter had stopped clicking each new amount. After checking the meter to view her fare, she opened her purse and counted out $4.30 plus a $1.00 tip.

"Thank you, Miss. Here's my card with my number. If you change your mind, call me, and I'll come back. There's a phone booth on that corner." He pointed in the direction. Cecilia's gaze followed the imaginary line to its destination, where a red booth sat near a park bench. An unshaved and shivering man wrapped in a threadbare blanket lay on the bench. "If you'll call me, I won't even charge you for the return ride. I know what they do in there."

She accepted his card, thanked him, and deposited it in her purse. He opened her door, and she stepped out clutching her purse. Mr. Woodson reached in, grabbed the small suitcase off the back seat, and handed it to her.

"I'll call you when I'm finished," she said in a determined, but soft voice. She stood straight, squared her thin shoulders, strode to the front door, and knocked.

A middle-aged woman wearing a stained uniform opened the door. "What's your name?" she asked in a gruff voice.

"My name is Cecilia Edmondson."

"You're late. Come in, Miss Edmondson. The doctor has been expecting you."

Cecilia turned her head and noted the taxi driver was still at the curb. She turned back to the woman and entered the dilapidated building.

*****

Two hours later, Cecilia awakened in a dim room. A single light bulb hung from the dingy high ceiling. A spider crawled across the molding between the ceiling and the wall to its web in the corner where it appeared to have caught a fly. At one time the room was probably painted white, but now it was a grimy gray. She was lying on a narrow cot. The gown they gave her barely covered her body. She straightened the gown, pulled it securely around her, and noticed the blood that soaked the sheet beneath her. She shuddered and looked around for someone.

On a nearby table some bloody rags filled a tray, along with a sharp-looking bloody metal instrument, and a pair of blood soaked gloves. A sink and a garbage can aligned one wall. Other than the cot, table, sink, and garbage can, the room was bare.

Cecilia had not known such fear in her eighteen years. *Why did I let Donna convince me that this was the right thing to do? Why didn't I talk to my parents?* She began to cry.

"Is there anybody out there?" she asked in a quivering voice. "Please help me." No one answered her cry for help. She asked again, and a tad louder. "Is anybody out there?" Her voice was the only sound in the nearly bare room, and it echoed back to her. No one came to her rescue.

With a sinking feeling, she slowly pushed herself to a sitting position, winced from the pain, and dangled her legs over the edge of the cot. She slid to her feet, balancing on the side of the cot, and the padding they stuffed between her legs fell to the floor. Feeling faint, she stood still for a moment. Her purse, suitcase, and coat lay on a makeshift shelf attached under the cot. She bent, grabbed her purse, and rummaged through it for her wallet. She let out a sigh of relief. *At least they were not thieves.* They only kept the money she had paid them. She opened the drawer in the table and found some rags that appeared clean.

On wobbly legs, she carried them to the sink and washed her body the best she could. She avoided peering into the trashcan, not wishing to see what it probably held. She returned to her suitcase, pulled out her clothes and dressed, padding her underpants with some of the remaining rags. Putting on her coat, she wondered what to do next, and then she remembered the card Mr. Woodson gave her. She rummaged through her purse and held it to her breast. *Thank you, God.* She took a deep breath. *Oh my, I just thanked God. As if He cares about me.*

Carrying the suitcase, Cecilia walked out of the room and on wobbly legs proceeded to the front entrance. She threw open the front door, and the sunlight blinded her in the dimly lit building. Turning around, she looked behind her to make sure no one was watching her, and although her body was in pain, she walked as fast as possible to the phone booth on the street corner. The homeless man on the bench was gone. Once inside, she closed the door, found a dime in her coin purse, and dialed the number with a trembling finger.

A female voice answered, "Woodson Taxi Service."

"I need to speak with Mr. Woodson. I was in his cab a few hours ago. I hope he can come and pick me up."

"I know who you are," the receptionist said in a soft, pleasant voice. "He said you might call. Hold on, Miss, and I'll go get him."

Within a minute, he answered. "Hello, this is Thomas Woodson."

"I need your help," Cecilia said nearly panicked. "Please pick me up as soon as possible. I'll be by the phone booth where you dropped me this morning."

"I'm on my way. Try to avoid strangers," he warned.

Cecilia stepped out of the phone booth. She looked in all directions but didn't see anyone. Although she was in pain, she began to pace and look at her watch. Ten minutes went by. Taking a seat on the vacated bench, she watched three little boys run out of the run-down house across the street, laughing and punching each other. One of the boys held a stick that probably once was a broom or mop handle. They formed a line in the street, and one boy pitched a ball to the one with the stick, and he hit it toward the third boy.

Another ten minutes went by, and several more boys joined the three. *I can tell they've done this many times before.* In spite of the chilly afternoon, the boys began a rousing game of stickball. They gathered three large rocks and used one manhole cover for the four bases.

While Cecilia waited, she watched the boys and thought about what she had done. *Was my baby going to be a boy or a girl? Would the baby have looked like me or like Ernie?*

"Stop it, Cecilia!" She berated herself out loud. "You can't change what you did, so quit thinking about what might have been. It just doesn't matter."

Some of the boys heard her and stopped to stare. She turned her back to them and spotted the taxi. Mr. Woodson stopped the cab, stepped out, and opened the rear door. She slid into the back seat, breathing heavily.

He sat back down in his seat and turned to her. "Are you all right?" he asked with genuine concern.

At that, the tears began to flow. Between sobs she managed to say, "I'm scared. The man and woman in there – they just left me."

"They always do, but they always return again.

Perhaps you should have waited," he said in a soft voice.

"I should probably go home, but I'm not ready to face my parents. I don't know what to do...."

"Would you like me to take you to the hospital?" he asked.

She thought for a moment. "Maybe. Do you know where I can go that's smaller ... like a clinic? I just need to make sure that I'm not bleeding to death."

"I can take you to my own doctor, if that works for you."

"That works." She gave him a slight smile. "Thank you, Mr. Woodson."

"You are welcome, Miss. I will pray for you on the drive there."

I probably need more than prayer. I don't think God will hear a prayer about me.

Chapter Two

Gloria

"For I the Lord thy God will hold thy right hand,
saying unto thee, Fear not; I will help thee."
Isaiah 41:13

Gary, Indiana
December 1, 1967
Gloria Reynolds signed her name on the registration sheet, and took a seat in the waiting room. She glanced around the room at those also here for the doctor. What stood out to her was the fact that she was the only woman alone. The pretty brunette directly across from her looked to be about five months pregnant. A man sat beside her with an arm draped over her shoulder. She looked into his eyes with such adoration when he spoke to her. Another woman appeared ready to give birth any day. She held her hand at the small of her back and grimaced. Her husband jumped up to request a pillow from the receptionist. Another man sat on a small stool in front of his grateful wife, and massaged her swollen ankles. All these couples wore wedding bands.

Gloria raised her head and blinked to hold back the tears. She fished a handkerchief from her purse to blow her nose. Leaning back in the chair, she closed her eyes, and inevitably thought of Matthew. After nearly an hour, she heard her name called. "*Miss* Gloria Reynolds." The nurse looked straight at her as she called her name. Gloria thought she emphasized the *Miss* much too loudly. Her name tag read Miss Redmond, RN.

Gloria was ushered into the examining room, handed a gown, and given some instructions. Within ten minutes Nurse Redmond returned, prepped her for the examination, and was a bit rough when she draped the sheet over Gloria, yanking it taught. The nurse did everything required in a cold-hearted way, and she lacked compassion. *She knows I'm unmarried. She reminds me of Nurse Ratched in the 1962 novel* "One Flew over the Cuckoo's Nest." *Nurse Redmond is insensitive, and I could picture Miss Redmond as a tyrant like Nurse Ratched.*

Gloria lay on the examination table, feet in stirrups, covered with a sheet, and waited for the doctor. His doctor's certificate with his picture hung on the wall along with several charts about the age progression of the child in the womb. A poster offered advice regarding pre-natal vitamins and the importance of good medical care throughout the pregnancy. Closing her eyes, she sighed loudly and thought of Matthew. She had not seen Matthew since early October, before he flew to Hawaii, and then on to Vietnam.

"Oh, Matthew, how I miss you," she said aloud. "I hope you're safe."

She realized the nurse and doctor could step in any moment and hear her talking to herself. It was enough humiliation possibly being pregnant, but she didn't want them thinking she was insane, too. She kept the remainder of her thoughts to herself.

I wish you were here, Matthew. I'm so scared. I hate this doctor's office. These people are so unpleasant. I was afraid and too embarrassed to go to my family doctor. I haven't told my parents my suspicions. I know they would be disappointed in us. I know you were heading on that fourteen day mission five weeks ago. I thought you would have written as soon as you returned. Maybe your letter was delayed. I know I'm being selfish about being scared. I can't imagine what you're going through in Vietnam. I love you so much.

She slipped one foot from the stirrup and reached toward the floor to retrieve her handkerchief from her purse, just as the doctor and the nurse entered. Forgetting the handkerchief, she quickly returned her foot to the stirrup. The nurse still maintained the stoic expression on her face, but the doctor smiled. She was hoping for an older doctor, not a handsome, blond Richard Chamberlain type, as in *Dr. Kildare*. Oh well, she was learning that you don't get all your wishes in life.

He looked at the chart in his hands. "Hello, Miss Reynolds. I'm Dr. Kessler. How are you this morning?" He flashed a pleasant bright white perfect teeth smile.

He not only looks like Dr. Kildare, but his name has to begin with a "K".

"I'm fine, Dr. Kil— I mean Kessler."

"I will examine you for the pregnancy determination you requested. Nurse Redmond will assist me. Do you have any questions before I begin?"

"No, sir." She did, but she didn't want to ask if there was an older doctor in the office. She was embarrassed enough, baring herself in front of a strange young man. She just wanted to get the examination over as fast as possible.

"Lay back and try to relax," he said, while washing his hands and arms.

Gloria lay flat on the table, but could not relax.

"I'll need to examine you internally, and I'll check your abdomen at the same time. This is to determine the size of your uterus and pelvis. This exam will also check for any abnormalities of the uterus, ovaries, or fallopian tubes." He held up his hands, Nurse Redmond dried them, and pulled the rubber gloves onto them snapping them in place.

Both of Gloria's fists clinched, and she bit her lips.

He began the examination, and talked calmly in a soft voice, while Nurse Redmond took notes. "Have you had other pregnancies?"

"No, sir."

"Have you had any surgeries?"

"I had my tonsils removed when I was four."

"Have you had any recent pain or soreness?"

"No, sir."

The examination did not take long; maybe seven or eight minutes at the most. "Okay, Miss Reynolds, I'm finished for now. You may get dressed, and I'll be back to speak with you." He removed his gloves, threw them into the trash receptacle, and again washed his hands. He left the room and Nurse Redmond followed, adding an icy glare toward Gloria before closing the door.

Gloria shivered, removed her feet from the stirrups, sat up on the examination table, and stepped down to the floor. She grabbed her jeans, sweater, and underclothes she had folded on the chair. Within five minutes she was dressed, and sitting in the chair when Doctor Kessler and Nurse Redmond returned.

"Miss Reynolds, I have determined that you are approximately eight weeks pregnant, and I'll set your due date on July 7, 1968. I have a prescription for pre-natal vitamins. Please fill this as soon as possible." He handed her the slip of paper. "Your blood pressure, heart and lungs are fine. You're young and healthy. You should have a successful pregnancy. I know you're not married, so if you consider having your baby adopted you may see my receptionist at the front desk for pamphlets on adoption agencies. I wish you all the best. Please schedule an appointment with me in three weeks. You can see my receptionist on the way out for that, too. God bless you, Miss Reynolds." At that, he and the Nurse Redmond turned and left the room.

Gloria sat staring at the door in a stupor. Finally she regained her thoughts. Doctor Kessler didn't mention the third option of abortion. If she chose abortion, she'd have to find a back-alley doctor or drive to one of the states it was now legal. Then she realized Dr. Kessler's last words: God bless you. *I don't think God cares about me at the moment. I know my parents won't either.*

Chapter Three

Loretta

"Therefore I will not refrain my mouth; I will speak in the anguish of my spirit; I will complain in the bitterness of my soul."
Job 7:11

Cincinnati, Ohio
December 1, 1967
Loretta Jenkins stared from her dorm window overlooking the campus of the University of Cincinnati. A man below walked around, tacking up signs inviting students to a Bible study that evening at seven o'clock. "*Me*, at a Bible study?" she scoffed aloud. "There's no God that cares ... at least about me." She jerked down the shade, closed the curtains, and shivered.

Walking to her closet, she chose a sweater folded on a shelf, and pulled it on over her blouse. "You'd think with the tuition cost, they could add some more heat in our rooms," she muttered. She sat at her desk to try and work on her history paper. There was a big test the next day, and she had barely studied.

Her mind wandered as she stared at the second bed in the room. Marianne Jones had been her roommate for the past two years, but she had recently moved into another room. Her only comments were, "I can no longer take your moodiness and attitude. You've changed, Loretta. You're not the sweet girl I knew."

Loretta's response only affirmed her roommate's choice. "Well, Miss Congeniality, I don't care for you either. You think you're so perfect. You don't know or care *anything* about me, and you *never* did. Go ahead and run out of here! See if I care!"

At that, Marianne had picked up her packed suitcase and walked out the door. Before leaving she turned and looked at Loretta with sad eyes, "You're wrong, Loretta. I *do* care about you. I just don't like how you've changed. I miss our—" Marianne never got a chance to finish her sentence because Loretta slammed the door in her face.

Now, Loretta was all alone with her thoughts. She sighed, leaned back on the rear two legs of the desk chair, and closed her eyes. *Maybe I should have been kinder to her. She was only trying to help. I just don't want anyone to know the truth. I need my mother. Why did my parents get killed in that car crash? I'd rather have my parents than the future inheritance. I'm not sure I even want to continue at UC. I'm so confused.*

The chair dropped with a loud thud, back onto all four legs, when a light knock sounded at the door. Loretta's head jerked toward the sound. At first she was frightened. Then she reprimanded herself. *Stop it, Loretta. Barry and his friends don't know which room is yours.*

Loretta didn't move, hoping the person would go away. No such luck. The person was insistent with a second knock that was much louder. She rose to her feet and slowly walked to the door. She looked through the peephole. *Oh, that's just great. It's that goody two-shoes Lydia Grace Wright. What could she possibly want from me?*

With reluctance, Loretta opened the door.

"Hi!" said Lydia Grace with a smile from ear-to-ear. "May I come in? I've got great news!"

"Sure, why not," said Loretta in a sarcastic tone, unenthused about any good news. What possible good news could this bubbly girl talk about ad nauseam to her?

Lydia Grace bounced in through the door and sat on the edge of the bed, doing her best to smooth her long brown curls, but to no avail. Loretta knew that on occasion Lydia Grace would iron the curls, so her hair would be poker straight, in the current style. Lydia Grace had those impeccable good looks: great cheekbones, a cute little nose, blue eyes that twinkled when she laughed, which was often, a dimple in each cheek, and a flawless complexion. She was tall, slender, graceful, and everyone loved her. She had a kind word for everybody. So here she was, perched on Loretta's bed, ready to spout the supposedly good news.

"I just spoke to our housemother. She said that two sisters are moving in, and would like to have a room to share. They're twins. She asked me if I would mind moving in with you, and I said I wouldn't mind at all. Since we have the same history, English, and music classes, we can help each other with homework. The twins can have my room, and I can room in here with you. My roommate returned home, so I was all alone. Now I get to room with someone I know from my classes. Isn't this great?" Lydia Grace flashed that big, famous smile, displaying her straight and even pearly white teeth.

Loretta just stared at her. *I can't believe this is happening. I knew I'd eventually be assigned a new roommate, but of all the possibilities, I didn't expect the perky, Barbie Doll, Bible-toting, Lydia Grace. Oh, good grief, why me?* Finally, Loretta was able to put the situation into perspective. She wasn't sure how to respond to Lydia Grace, but the housemother would just assign someone else if Loretta didn't accept Lydia Grace. Loretta sighed and asked, "When are you moving in?"

"Tonight, right after the Bible study. I'm already packed, and I've cleaned my room. Would you like to attend the Bible study with me? It would be like having a fourth class together." Lydia Grace looked at Loretta with such expectation that Loretta almost hated to dash her hopes. However, she soon recovered from the agreeable mood.

"No, I *don't* want to go to the Bible study with you, and please don't ask me again. Let me set you straight, Lydia Grace. I'm not into all that nonsense. Please keep your thoughts about God to yourself, and we'll get along just fine."

Lydia Grace looked as though a bucket of water had been thrown in her face. At last she stammered, "Okay, I ... will respect ... your feelings. I'll see you around eight-thirty. Okay?"

"Sure, fine."

Lydia Grace rose and walked to the door. She turned around, and started to say something else, but obviously changed her mind. She opened the door and left.

Loretta locked the door, turned on the radio, and lay down on her bed. "Silence is Golden" by The Tremeloes played. "How appropriate," she muttered out loud. She stared up at the ceiling, and tears ran down her cheeks, dropping into her ears. "Oh, Mom," she wailed, "why did you and Dad have to die? I need you so much. I've turned into the sort of person I used to despise, but I can't seem to help myself. Oh, why did I ever go to that frat party? I was so dumb and naïve. I can't have a baby. I've got my whole life ahead of me. Oh, Mom, if you were only here."

The tears fell, and the history test was long forgotten. She listened to the lyrics of the song that fit so well. *"How could she tell he deceived her so well? Pity she'll be the last one to know."*

Chapter Four

Mr. and Mrs. Woodson

*"And to godliness brotherly kindness; and to
brotherly kindness charity."*
2 Peter 1:7

Houston, Texas
December 8, 1967
Cecilia Edmonson awakened to the smell of coffee
and frying bacon. In the dim light, she stretched
her arms and focused on the clock on the
nightstand. Six o'clock. *I must say that this family
is always punctual.* For the past week, everything
was on an organized schedule – like her own
family. She knew that at this moment, Mrs.
Woodson was cooking with her oldest daughter Jill.
The three younger children were sitting at the
breakfast table, while they all listened to Mr.
Woodson read from his Bible.

The whole family would be dressed and ready
for the day. The children walked to school at exactly
seven-thirty, and at the same time Mr. Woodson
left for work in his taxi. She had been staying in

their home since the evening of December first. She thought back to that day when the taxi driver picked her up at the phone booth ... following the abysmal experience.

Mr. Woodson had driven her to Dr. Livingston, a kind man in his early fifties. Both men, she learned, were deacons in the same church. Although Dr. Livingston knew what she had done, he did not chastise her. He checked her thoroughly, started her on antibiotics, and told her he wanted to see her in one week to make certain she was healing as expected. He warned her that if she began to hemorrhage, she was to go into the emergency room at the nearest hospital immediately. If that happened, she was to ask the nurse on duty to call him, and he would be there for her.

As they walked to the taxi following her visit with Dr. Livingston, Mr. Woodson had asked, "Are you ready to go home and see your parents?"

She recalled hanging her head, shaking it in the negative. "I still can't face them. Please just drive me to a cheap motel nearby. I'll call you in one week to drive me to Dr. Livingston's office." She lifted her chin and looked up into his kind eyes. "I appreciate all you've done for me. Thank you."

He had studied her face. "I know your first name is Cecilia. I overheard some of the conversation, when you gave your name to the nurse. May I call you Cecilia?"

"Yes, you may."

"Alice is my wife. I would like to invite you to come and stay with us, for now. I want you to know that I have never invited anyone into my home who has been in my taxi, but you look like you could use a friend. Alice is a delightful and loving woman, and we have four fine children. My oldest child Jill is only a couple of years younger than you."

She had placed her hand on his arm and stopped him. "Mr. Woodson, I appreciate the offer, but I don't want to put you and your family out. I will be fine at the motel."

"As you wish, but you would not be an imposition to us. I'll drive you to the nearest motel. It's only a couple of miles from here."

Cecilia had sat in silence as he drove. The well-lit sign advertised the name of the motel as Weary Traveler's Rest Stop, and a neon sign intermittently flashed Vacancy. When they pulled into the parking lot, there were three other cars parked a fair distance from the office. Three young men and three young women sat on the hoods of the cars, drinking beer, smoking pot, laughing, and kissing.

Cecilia had scrutinized them in quiet reflection. A couple of months ago that was her, but not now. She stared out the taxi window, and Mr. Woodson turned in his seat to face her. Cecilia knew he saw her expression and the tear that trailed down her cheek. He asked again in a gentle voice, "Cecilia, it's no burden on my family. I would really like for you to stay with us, and for as long as you like."

She turned to him and studied his kind face. She knew she didn't want to be around kids such as these again. All she wanted was to rest and heal. She also feared that she could be tempted to go back to her "summer of love" ways. She needed more time to get her head on straight.

When at last she spoke, her voice trembled. "I would be pleased to stay with you and your family, Mr. Woodson. Thank you," she said as she wiped away the tear.

He had turned around in his seat, and before she could change her mind, they drove to his home. He introduced her to his wife, and Alice Woodson welcomed her.

*****

Cecilia had now been at the Woodson home a week, and today was the day to return to Dr. Livingston's office. She had been taking her antibiotics on schedule, and felt no complications. She expected a clean bill of health.

She dressed, brushed her teeth, and combed her long blonde hair, pulling it back into a ponytail. She looked into the mirror on the bathroom wall and washed the sleep from her eyes. Her dad's slanted pale blue eyes stared back at her, and she felt a twinge of homesickness.

She entered the kitchen. Mr. Woodson was still reading his Bible aloud, and she whispered to Mrs. Woodson, "May I set the table?"

"Yes, dear."

Cecilia busied herself setting the table, but could not help from hearing what Mr. Woodson was reading.

"'And he said unto me, My grace is sufficient for thee: for my strength is made perfect in weakness. Most gladly therefore will I rather glory in my infirmities, that the power of Christ may rest upon me. Therefore I take pleasure in infirmities, in reproaches, in necessities, in persecutions, in distresses for Christ's sake: for when I am weak, then am I strong.'" He looked up from his Bible. "That's from Second Corinthians chapter twelve and verses nine and ten."

Mrs. Woodson and Jill served the food, and Mr. Woodson closed the Bible. Cecilia thought about what he'd read. *I've been weak. Would He give me strength? No, not me. I'm undeserving. I've probably hurt my parents and little brothers. I know they're in pain, but I still can't face them.*

"Cecilia," said Mrs. Woodson.

Cecilia turned to her, "Yes, ma'am?"

"What time is your doctor's appointment?"

"It's at nine o'clock."

"Well, as soon as the children leave for school, and Mr. Woodson leaves for work, we can wash the dishes, and I will drive you."

"Thank you, Mrs. Woodson."

*****

They arrived at Dr. Livingston's office a little before nine. Mrs. Woodson parked the car and smiled at Cecilia. "Cecilia would you like me to go into the examination room with you?" she gently asked.

Cecilia looked into the kind, motherly face. For a brief second she wished Mrs. Woodson was her own mom. Cecilia returned the smile and responded with, "I'd like that, Mrs. Woodson."

Cecilia gave her name to the receptionist and waited with Mrs. Woodson. Within fifteen minutes, her name was called. A nurse handed her a gown, with instructions to lie down on the table with her feet in the stirrups. Mrs. Woodson draped the sheet neatly over Cecilia. Within ten minutes the nurse returned with Dr. Livingston.

Following the examination, Dr. Livingston asked Cecilia to dress and he would return.

He reentered her room with a solemn expression on his face, while pulling up a chair. He cleared his throat and looked her in the eye. "Cecilia, what I am about to say ... please, I don't want to sound like I'm lecturing you. However, I would be remiss in my doctor's oath if I didn't explain a few facts to you. You're a very lucky young lady. So many things could have happened to you, even if you had received a legal abortion in a clean and authorized abortion clinic in Colorado, California, Oregon or North Carolina: the states that currently allow abortions under certain conditions. I'm sure you were *not* informed, or maybe I should say warned, that women have died from infection, tearing of the cervix muscles or ripping of the uterine wall. The abortion could affect future pregnancies. You could have a permanent weakening of your cervix, which would result in your cervix not being able to carry the weight of another pregnancy. If that happens, you will not be able to carry another child to term. This scenario is more frequent with women eighteen and under, and I know you are eighteen. I am telling you this so that you know the facts before considering another abortion."

Cecilia could only blink and stare at the doctor. No, she had not been told any of the dangers. All she knew was that she wanted rid of the problem and as soon as possible. She was not certain how far along she was, but knew it was probably within three months. *The first trimester wasn't really a baby ... was it?*

"I'm also going to leave you with this pamphlet showing the developmental stages of the unborn child from conception through birth. If you decide to stay in town, please schedule an appointment with me in two to three weeks. If you don't stay in town, please schedule with another doctor for a follow-up. I wish you all the best, Cecilia," he said, as he made his exit.

Cecilia was quiet on the drive back to the Woodsons' home. All she wanted to do was go to bed and bury her thoughts. She had not looked at the pamphlet, but shoved it to the bottom of her purse.

On the return drive, Mrs. Woodson allowed her the time alone with her thoughts. Cecilia did not come downstairs for lunch or dinner. Around seven o'clock, Cecilia's stomach began to growl. She knew she should eat something. She had not slept all day, but lay on the bed and thought about her future. She wasn't ready to face her parents, but she also didn't want to alarm them further. She knew she needed to at least telephone them. However, she wasn't sure she could do that either. She had not seen them since she left home with Ernie on graduation day, June fourth.

She and Ernie had planned this escape since mid-May. They wanted to be free from obligations. They had heard about all the fun which kids their age and even younger were having on their own. They had no responsibilities in the Haight-Ashbury neighborhood of San Francisco. They had freedom to do as they pleased. They were both tired of their parents, their church, and they had no intention of going to college. They left on Ernie's 1960 Harley-Davidson motorcycle with only a one-line note to her parents. *School is over, and I'm hitting the road with Ernie.* He said about the same thing in his goodbye note to his parents.

*****

Cecilia opened her bedroom door, tiptoed down the hallway to the top of the steps, and sat down. She could see from where she sat that the television was on, and the family had tuned into *Tarzan* on NBC. She heard them laugh at the antics of Boy and Cheetah. She remained seated and studied them. They were a loving family, but so was hers. Her parents were Christians, just like this family. *I've gone so far astray. I'm not sure what I should do. I need time to think ... but where? I can't continue to stay here – or go home.*

Sarah, the younger Woodson daughter, turned and saw her. "Come on down and watch *Tarzan* with us, Cecilia."

They all turned and urged her to join them. Cecilia descended the stairs and took a seat in one of the available chairs. "Would you like something to eat? I saved you a plate," said Mrs. Woodson.

"Yes, ma'am. Thank you. I'll help."

Cecilia was hungry, but she ate slowly, while both Mr. and Mrs. Woodson sat at the table with her. When she finished eating, she carried her plate to the sink, rinsed it, and set it in the dishwasher.

"Are you okay, Cecilia?" asked Mrs. Woodson. "I know that today's visit with the doctor was difficult for you."

Cecilia sat back down. She could hear the children in the living room enjoying the program. It seemed like ages since she was able to watch television. Her innocence was gone. She wondered if she would ever be happy again.

"I'm fine," was her vague answer to the question.

Mr. Woodson looked toward Mrs. Woodson, and she nodded in answer to his silent question.

They held hands as he spoke to Cecilia. "Do you feel as though you can go home, yet?" he asked her.

She squirmed in her seat. She wasn't sure how to answer. *Are they tired of me? Did they want me to leave? Maybe they feel I'm a bad influence on their daughters. If so, it's definitely understandable.*

"If I've worn out my welcome, please tell me," she said pointedly.

Mrs. Woodson interrupted. "It's not that, dear.

You definitely haven't worn out your welcome. We are both concerned for your happiness and your future. As parents, we also know your parents are probably very worried about you. When did you last speak to them?"

Cecilia had not revealed any information about her past summer. She felt too ashamed to tell the Woodsons. They might not want to help her if they knew. She took a deep breath. "I graduated from Memorial Senior High School on June fourth this year. It was the last day I saw or spoke to my parents. After the ceremony, my boyfriend Ernie and I ran away. We'd heard things about the Haight-Ashbury neighborhood of San Francisco, and thought we'd like the adventure. Ernie and I split up in late September. He hit the road, but I stayed in San Francisco until mid-October. I suspected I might be pregnant, and I wanted to go home, or at least return to Houston. But when I got here, I knew I couldn't go back to my parents, so I crashed not too far from here at a school friend's apartment. She and her boyfriend live together. She was the one who gave me the address and phone number for the abortion doctor. You know the rest."

She studied their faces, but neither one showed signs of disgust. They only showed compassion. Mrs. Woodson was the first to speak. She placed her hand on Cecilia's. "I still need to know if you are ready to go home."

Cecilia stared into the sympathetic face. "I'm not. However, I know I should move on. I just don't know where. I need time to collect my thoughts. I know I don't want to stay in Houston. I need to get away, but I don't want to go back to San Francisco either. I need some time alone to think."

Mr. Woodson spoke next. "My wife and I have discussed your dilemma. We want to help, and we know a place where you can go. We think it will help you. It's where we honeymooned in nineteen forty-seven." He picked up his wife's hand and smiled lovingly at her. "It's a special place any time of the year, but even more special during the Christmas season. It's called Christmas Hotel, and it's located in the quaint and friendly little town of Franklin, Kentucky. The proprietors are an amazing couple. People don't only stay there for honeymoons, although that was wonderful for us." He kissed Mrs. Woodson's hand. "They also go there to find rest, and find healing for their spirits. I think you might find a Christmas miracle if you go. If you don't have enough money, our church has a benevolence fund. As a deacon, I will put in a request to have our church finance your journey and your stay. Would you like that, Cecilia?"

Cecilia regarded their kind faces and began to

cry. "Why would you do that for me? I am undeserving ... of ... your generosity." She choked out the words between sobs.

Mrs. Woodson moved her chair closer to hold Cecilia. She patted Cecilia's back and let her cry it out. "There, there, child," she said soothingly. She pulled away, handed Cecilia a tissue, and cupped Cecilia's face in her hands. "You'll be okay. You're strong. You'll find your way back."

Cecilia wiped her eyes and blew her nose. *I'm not so sure.*

Chapter Five

MIA

*"Have mercy upon me, O Lord, for I am in
trouble: mine eye is consumed with grief,
yea, my soul and my belly."*
Psalms 31:9

Gary, Indiana
December 8, 1967
Gloria Reynolds sat in the living room in the home
where she had lived all her life. She picked up a
pillow and hugged it to her, preparing for the
inevitable interrogation. Her parents Ralph and
Irene sat on the sofa across from her.

"Do you plan on attending college for the next
semester?" asked her mother. "If you do, you need
to apply soon, before all the classes are filled. Your
father and I just don't want you to waste your life in
menial work."

Her dad took over the discussion. "You can't
keep moping around the house. We love Matthew,
too, but he's in the army and doing something with
his life. He would expect you to begin your life's

purpose. Don't you want to become a nurse anymore? It was always your dream ever sense you were little. Have you lost that desire?"

She glanced from her dad to her mom. She loved them both so much, and how could she possibly tell them that they would be grandparents in seven months, unless she aborted it. They were going to be so disappointed in her. She knew they were worried about her. Her parents were so perfect in her eyes. Although, they had gone all through school together, they didn't date until her dad returned from Germany in 1945, after the war ended. They fell in love, married a year later, and she was their only child, born October 8, 1949.

Matthew's father, Pastor Warren Johnson, was the preacher at the First Baptist Church of Gary, Indiana. Matthew's mother Bertha played the organ for the services. Gloria's father was a deacon in the Johnsons' church, and Gloria's mother held the position of church secretary. Both sets of parents had grown up together and were best friends. They wed in a double ceremony, and both couples honeymooned together.

They often described and remembered with affection Christmas Hotel in Franklin, Kentucky, where they spent their joint honeymoon. Gloria couldn't imagine sharing a honeymoon with another couple, but that's what her parents and the

Johnsons did. After they were married, they even bought houses next door to each other. Like Gloria, Matthew was the Johnsons' only child, born the day before Gloria.

Gloria took a deep breath and exhaled. "Yes, I still hope to become a nurse. I just don't think the time is quite right. I need more time."

"You need more time?" asked her father. "I don't understand. I know you miss Matthew, but you have to get on with your life. I don't think Matthew wants you to put yourself on hold for him while he's in Vietnam. Is there something you're not telling us?"

Gloria stared into her father's eyes, and then shifted her gaze. She knew he was so good at "reading" her. She feared he would figure out her dilemma before she had the nerve to tell him … to tell them both. Therefore, in answer to his question, she lied.

"No, I have nothing to tell you, Daddy." She stood and walked to the window and pulled back the drapes. She needed to escape the interrogation. An official-looking car pulled up at the front curb of the Johnsons' house next door. Two men in army uniform got out and strode to the Johnsons' front door. Gloria turned back to her parents. She felt the blood drain from her face as her knees buckled.

"There are two men in uniform at the Johnsons'

door," she gasped. Then she fainted and fell to the floor.

When she revived, her mother wiped Gloria's face with a cold cloth, and her father held her hand. "Please help me up," she said in panic. "I need to go next door."

Gloria was determined and impatient when they did not help her immediately. "I need to go *now*!"

Her father pulled her to her feet. On wobbly legs, she balanced with the aid of her father.

"We'll go with you," said her mother.

Pastor Johnson opened the door to their knock. His face was ashen. Gloria looked past him to Mrs. Johnson, who was sitting on the sofa crying, while the two men sat in chairs near her and continued to speak softly to her.

Gloria burst through the door, and fell to her knees on the floor in front of Mrs. Johnson. The two women embraced and the officers stood.

Pastor Johnson lightly touched Gloria's shoulder and spoke in a hushed, but hoarse voice. "He's not dead, Gloria. His status is missing in action, or MIA." He turned back to the representatives of the United States Army. "Allow me to introduce Matthew's fiancée Gloria Reynolds, and her parents Ralph and Irene Reynolds."

Gloria stood, and she and her parents shook hands with the men who introduced themselves as

Lt. Col. James Cambridge and Captain Robert Montgomery.

"If you don't mind, please repeat to Gloria what you told us," said Pastor Johnson. He brought two chairs from the dining room for the Reynolds, and he indicated to the Reynolds family and the officers to have a seat. Pastor Johnson, then took a seat on the sofa by his wife, and Gloria sat on his wife's other side.

Lt. Col. Cambridge spoke first. "Miss Reynolds, we will explain to you what we are authorized. Some of the information is classified. Your fiancé Private E-2 Matthew Johnson was with the EMU. As you are probably aware, EMU stands for Experimental Military Unit. EMU joined with the United States Army's 135th Assault Helicopter Company with a contingent of the Royal Australian Navy. On October thirtieth, the helicopter your fiancé was in came under heavy fire, but the pilot managed to make a controlled crash landing. Another of our helicopters was able to land and pick up three of the badly injured men. We don't know at this moment the fate of your fiancé. We know he wasn't with his helicopter when rescue arrived. The crash happened in North Vietnam territory, but he was not reported captured in a POW camp, so he is listed as MIA. I wish I could tell you more, but that is the only information available to us at this time."

Gloria stared into his kind face. She felt the tears roll down her face. Mrs. Johnson handed her the tissue box she held on her lap. Gloria looked down at the box, removed a tissue, and handed the box back.

"Why did it take so long to let us know?" asked Gloria, rather bluntly and clearly disturbed. "That was five weeks ago!"

"I'm sorry, but the mission was top secret, and we still had hopes of finding him. That's all I can report at this time."

As if in a mindless daze, Gloria stared at the wall behind the officers as she wiped her face and eyes. She found herself looking at a collage of pictures on the wall. They were all of Matthew, some with her, and she had studied them many times. Matthew when he was born, Matthew at age fourteen months, walking barefoot on the grass and laughing. She and Matthew playing in the sand box at the park at age two, and another picture of Matthew at age four learning to swim at the local pool. One of her favorite pictures was of Matthew at age six entering the elementary school for his first day of school, holding his mother's hand. He looked so vulnerable, unlike the man he later grew into.

There were several more pictures at different ages, and then three with her. A picture of them dressed for the junior prom, and another going to the senior prom. Matthew was so handsome with his dark brown hair and brown eyes. The final two pictures were of Matthew in his dress uniform following boot camp, the day he left for Vietnam. He had his arm around Gloria in the second picture.

These two pictures were taken the morning after her eighteenth birthday. The night before, they held their own secret wedding ceremony at their favorite spot up on the highest point overlooking the city. They spoke beautiful vows to God, and that they would love each other forever. Before God, they pronounced themselves man and wife. They conceived their baby that night. In their hearts they were married.

Gloria was pulled from her reverie with a discreet clearing of the throat by her father. She looked at her dad. Her eyes were probably red and swollen, but she didn't care. No doubt, they were all awaiting a response from her. All she could manage was a thank you to the officers. Gloria rose to her feet, hugged Mr. and Mrs. Johnson, and took her leave with her parents.

*****

The next morning, Gloria didn't want to get out of bed. She slept fitfully, tossing and turning all night, deliberating whether to tell her parents about the pregnancy. At the moment she didn't want to speak of it. Matthew was missing in action, and she only wanted to discuss the situation with him. She now wondered if keeping the baby was a valid option, although it was a part of Matthew. There was adoption and abortion to consider. A decision had to be made, and soon, while it was still just plasma.

She rose, wrapped her robe around herself, and slipped into her house shoes. Although tired and depressed, Gloria knew she needed to speak to her parents. She viewed herself in the vanity mirror, and the face that looked back appeared ten years older than the day before. Her amber eyes were still swollen and red, and there were bags underneath.

She entered the bathroom and walked to the sink where she splashed water on her face, brushed her teeth, and then combed her long straight golden brown hair, parting it neatly down the center. She had been pleased with her hair. It was right in style, and she didn't have to iron it to straighten it. However, at the moment, she didn't care about fashion.

She returned to her bedroom, pulled on her bellbottom jeans, a sweater, her gym shoes and socks, and then descended the stairs and headed into the kitchen where her parents would be having their morning coffee at the kitchen table. That had been their ritual as far back as Gloria could remember.

When she opened the swinging door that separated the dining room from the kitchen, they stopped speaking when she entered. "Would you like a cup of coffee?" asked her mother, jumping up.

"Yes, please."

Her mother set the steaming mug of black coffee in front of her, and she sat back down beside her father. It was piping hot and black, just as her parents and she liked their coffee. She took a sip, wrapping both hands around the hot mug. It was comforting. Finally she looked at her parents. With a huge sigh she began.

"My heart is broken, as I know your hearts are, too. I didn't sleep much last night, and I couldn't pray. I realize I'm depressed and scared, but I don't know how to get over this funk I'm in." The tears began again. Her mother handed her a box of tissues. She took one and wiped her eyes and cheeks. "Just when I think I can't possibly have any more tears to cry, here they come again."

Her dad nodded. "What can we do to help, honey? We love you, and if *you* can't pray, I want you to know that your mother and I have been praying for the three of us – and for Matthew and his parents."

She glared back at him. Raising her voice in

anger she asked, "What good is prayer? Will prayer bring Matthew home? Will prayer heal my heart? Does God really care about me? You two raised me to believe God was love. Where is *His* love now? Where is *His* mercy? Why would a *good* God allow this to happen? Matthew and I just turned eighteen. We had our whole lives ahead of us. God is not a *just* God! He's an *unjust* God! I no longer want to be referred to as a Christian!" She slammed her fist down on the table in defiance, and her face colored red in rage.

Her mother began to cry. Her father responded to her tirade. "Oh, Gloria, you can't possibly mean all that. You know better. God knows where Matthew is, and He has his reasons. In a few days you'll feel differently, and you'll be able to pray again. God *does* love you. You mustn't speak like that."

"I can speak any way I want!" She rose so abruptly that her chair fell over behind her. She picked it up and announced, "I'm going for a walk. I need to be alone."

"Gloria, we love you," her father said with compassion and tears in his eyes.

She looked back at him and lowered her voice. "I know you both love me." Gloria's gaze shifted to her mother. "I love you both, too." She ran her fingers through her hair. "I need some fresh air. I need to decide what to do. I have some things to sort out; decisions to make."

She grabbed her wool car coat from the front hall closet, and was out the door before they could say another word.

She stepped out on the front porch and took a deep breath, noting the swing and the two rockers. Her parents spent many summer nights in those rockers holding hands. She and Matthew had spent many nights in the swing. Her parents and his parents called it courting, and both sets of parents approved of the courtship.

She walked to the edge of the porch, looked up and sniffed the air. A cold front had moved in last night, and the air held a brisk chill. She buttoned her coat, reached in her pockets for her gloves and knit hat, and walked down the steps as she pulled on her hat and gloves. She decided to head to the park where she and Matthew had spent many days as small children and sweethearts.

When she entered the park's grounds, she then followed the pathway toward the children's area. She approached the swings and sat on one and began to swing. She pushed higher and higher until her long hair, hanging underneath the knit hat, whipped around her face. She let her mind go blank. She didn't want to think, so she closed her eyes to block out everything around her, and just let the cold air bite her face. She heard someone speak her name. When Gloria opened her eyes and looked down, she saw Mrs. Ferguson from church, with her twin boys in the double stroller.

"Hello, Gloria," she called out, and waved.

Gloria returned the wave.

"How's Matthew?" asked Mrs. Ferguson.

"Okay," Gloria lied.

"I'll see you at church on Sunday," and she walked on.

Gloria was thankful Mrs. Ferguson didn't hang around. She didn't want a conversation. It was in that moment she knew she must get away. If she stayed in Gary, Indiana, people would keep asking about Matthew, and she didn't want to answer their questions. She thought about where she would go. Using her feet to stop the swing, she looked around the play yard. There was the sandbox she and Matthew played in as children. Her eyes moved to the see-saw and the four-square court. On the tennis court a young couple played tennis, even though it was cold. They wore sweat pants and ski jackets. They were probably in love.

She and Matthew had done foolish things, too. Everywhere she looked, she saw bits and pieces of her years with Matthew. They had been so in love, just like her parents and his parents when they married. Then a startling thought crossed her mind, and she realized where she would go for the peace and quiet she needed.

Yes, she needed to get away. Gloria jogged as she left the park. She encountered two more people she knew, but avoiding any conversation, she just said "hi" and rushed past.

She hurried up the porch steps and entered the house, inhaling deeply the aroma of breakfast cooking: bacon and eggs. She hung up her coat and stuffed the hat and gloves back into the pockets. She walked into the kitchen, kissed her mom and dad on the cheek, and washed her hands at the sink. They turned to her with surprised expressions on their faces.

"After breakfast, I'm going to pack and go away for a while. I need to be alone. I won't be able to stomach speaking with people and answering questions about Matthew."

Her parents did not appear surprised. Gloria suspected they were expecting this decision. After a brief pause her dad asked, "Where will you go?"

"I'm going to the place you two and the Johnsons found special. I'm going to Christmas Hotel."

Her parents turned to each other. Relieved, she recognized the pleased and knowing expression in their smiles. She wouldn't need to fight them about her decision.

Chapter Six

Christmas Vacation

*"She openeth her mouth with wisdom;
and in her tongue is the law of kindness."*
Proverbs 31:26

Cincinnati, Ohio
December 8, 1967
Bubbly Lydia Grace had invaded Loretta's space. Loretta tried to avoid her, but it was impossible. Not only did they have three classes together, but Lydia Grace would spend an hour each morning, and an hour each evening studying her Bible in their room. Sometimes she'd encourage a Biblical discussion with Loretta.

Loretta tried being rude to Lydia Grace, but it didn't seem to deter her. Lydia Grace would just smile, then return to her Bible. Oftentimes she would sing hymns. Loretta had to admit that Lydia Grace had a beautiful soprano voice, and she played the piano quite well. Having taken piano lessons from her father since she was eight, and proficient with several other musical instruments, she was here at the University of Cincinnati in the Conservatory of Music Department on a music scholarship.

Loretta remembered when her temperament was like Lydia Grace, back when her days were carefree and she enjoyed life. That was before the car accident on October first and the frat party on October seventh. Loretta knew that she'd never have gone to that party if her parents had lived. Her parents were her rock, and in one quick moment they were both gone. If she'd been in her right mind, she would never have put herself in a situation in which Barry could force himself upon her as he did. *Dumb and naïve, I was, but nevermore.*

It was Friday morning, and school would be out for Christmas vacation one week from today. She didn't want to stay at the school during that period, and chance running into Barry and his frat brothers. She had nowhere to go, and would have to make a decision soon. If only she had an aunt or uncle or some cousins who lived close. Donald, her brother, was in the air force and currently stationed in Germany. He came home for their parents' funeral, but had to return to Germany immediately following. Separated in age by ten years, Loretta hardly knew him.

She walked into the bathroom she shared with

Lydia Grace, removed the jumbo curlers from her hair, and brushed her thick collar-length shiny black hair into the long smooth bob. She then teased her bangs that hung just over her eyebrows. Her hair had always been her best feature. Her eyes were dark brown, almost black like her hair, and she stood little more than five foot with an hourglass figure. However, she had always wanted to be tall and slender like Lydia Grace. Loretta had left the door open, so she wasn't surprised when Lydia Grace appeared in the doorway.

"Loretta, do you have anywhere to go for Christmas vacation?"

Loretta didn't know what to say. Lydia Grace knew about her parents' death, and Donald stationed overseas. "I thought I might hang out around here. I can get caught up on the next history paper due January fifteenth."

"Well, I wrote my parents, and they agreed that if you'd like, we'd all love to have you stay with us at our home in Franklin, Kentucky. Or you can stay at Christmas Hotel, which is nearby, if you'd rather be alone. You can always catch up on the paper there. Perhaps we can even work on our papers together. What do you say?"

Loretta thought about the offer. She knew she didn't want to chance seeing Barry or his frat friends. There would be very few students not going home, so if Barry and his friends remained on campus she would be easily spotted. She could not think of where else she could go. Staying at Christmas Hotel wouldn't be so bad. She would have her privacy. From Lydia Grace's descriptions, she knew Christmas Hotel was quite an amazing place. She made her decision.

"Thank you. I would like to go to Franklin with you."

Chapter Seven

Christmas Hotel

*"And let us not be weary in well doing: for in due
season we shall reap, if we faint not."*
Galatians 6:9

Monday, December 11, 1967
Cecilia arrived in Franklin, Kentucky late in the
afternoon. Her legs were cramped and unsteady
from the long bus ride, and the internal wounds
from her abortion still brought some pain. She
pulled her overnight bag from the overhead
compartment and followed the other passengers
down the steps to the sidewalk. The baggage
department in the side of the bus was open, and she
waited her turn to retrieve her luggage. Thanks to
the good people at the Woodsons' church, she had
enough new clothes to fill a small suitcase.

While she waited, she listened to the chatter of
the other passengers. A young couple held the hand
of a toddler, and discussed how happy they were to
be home in Franklin for Christmas. Another woman
soothed a crying infant, patting the baby as he lay

on her shoulder, while her husband retrieved their luggage. Another couple laughed and teased their three little girls, entertaining them with funny facial expressions while they waited in line for their luggage.

Each family appeared happy and loving. Yes, family was the key word. They were a family, and it had been a long time since Cecilia felt part of a family. She turned her head away from the people, no longer wanting to watch, and pulled her coat tighter. The temperature was around sixty-five degrees when she left Houston, Texas, but it was probably about thirty here in Franklin, Kentucky. The wind blew, and she shivered.

Finally, it was her turn. She handed the claim ticket to a man who in turn handed her the suitcase. "Here you go, Miss. Enjoy your stay in Franklin!"

"Thank you." She spun around and walked toward the bus station. When she entered the building, she spotted a little diner, and walked up to a pretty brunette waitress behind the counter. On her uniform a plastic name tag read Carol Ann.

"Hi, I'm new in Franklin," said Cecilia. "Would you please tell me how to get to Christmas Hotel?"

"That's no problem, honey," she said in her soft southern drawl. "You can actually see part of it from here." The hospitable waitress escorted Cecilia to the front door where she pointed her finger. "Just walk in that direction, honey, and you'll see it on the corner of North Main and East Cedar Street. You can't miss it. It's magnificent."

"Thank you." *Southern charm is certainly not lost on the people of this town.*

Cecilia entered the town's square. She checked out the businesses, all decorated with Christmas wreathes, and the courthouse in the square dressed up, also. All the light poles were wrapped in pine garland, with red bows attached near the top. Mr. and Mrs. Woodson were right about Franklin, then and now. *It's a very pretty town.*

Cecilia's legs ached, and she had not had much sleep on the bus. She flopped down on the nearest bench and set her purse, suitcase, and overnight bag near her. In her overnight bag was a letter of introduction from Mr. and Mrs. Woodson. She opened the case, retrieved the envelope containing the letter, and the check from the church for $300 made out to Christmas Hotel. She opened the envelope and reread the letter.

December 8, 1967

Dear Christopher and Jerilyn Wright,
I'm sure you probably won't remember us,
but we stayed at Christmas Hotel on our

honeymoon in 1947. We have considered many times about returning for a vacation, but then the children began to arrive. We now have four lovely children, and it's difficult to find the time. Maybe someday we'll just bring the whole family at Christmas time.

In the meantime, we would like to introduce Miss Cecilia Edmondson from our hometown of Houston, Texas. She's a lovely young lady, but has had some unhappiness in the past six months. I know of no better place to rest and heal than at Christmas Hotel. Our church is sponsoring her stay with you out of our benevolence fund. If the amount of money we sent with her is not enough, please just bill us for the remainder. At this time, Miss Edmondson does not know how long she will be staying.

Yours truly,

Thomas and Alice Woodson

Cecilia refolded the letter from the Houston taxi driver and his wife and placed it back in the envelope with the check. She looked up as a small single-engine prop aircraft flew overhead, momentarily disturbing the quietness of the town. She sighed and closed her eyes. She needed to check in to the hotel, but she just wasn't in a hurry. It was cold, and she began to shiver again.

"Are you all right, Miss?"

Cecilia opened her eyes, startled. She looked into the strange man's kind eyes. "I'm fine. I just needed to rest for a minute."

"I'd be happy to carry your suitcase. Are you heading to Christmas Hotel?" The young man pointed across the street and down a few buildings. This was her first glance at the hotel, and it *was* magnificent. She recognized that the brick building was quite old, but definitely well-maintained. It was five stories tall, with CHRISTMAS HOTEL carved into a massive stone block near the top of the fifth story. Just below this she could read another carving, also in stone: WHERE JESUS' BIRTH IS A DAILY CELEBRATION.

The two stories high, massive double glass and brass trimmed doors were recessed about twenty inches into the building. Two angels, carved into the façade adjacent to each brass trimmed door, gave an unusual but very welcoming feature. Below the right-hand angel, she noticed a brass plaque inscribed with the date 1850. Gas coach lights shone an orange glow from above onto both angels.

She turned back to the well-groomed, dark haired, clean shaved, and handsome young man; so unlike Ernie. He responded with a slow smile and a heavy Southern drawl. "I suspect this is your first view of Christmas Hotel. Folks around here just take it for granted. It's nice seeing it through the eyes of someone new in town. By the way, my name is Eugene Scott." He held out his hand.

Cecilia took it, and they shook hands. She noticed his trimmed and clean fingernails.

"My name is Cecilia Edmondson, and you're correct. I'm on my way to Christmas Hotel, and I am new in town."

"Well, Cecilia, I'm happy to make your acquaintance." His blue eyes twinkled when he smiled.

"I'm happy to make your acquaintance, too, Eugene," and she returned the smile. *Everyone I meet is polite and welcoming.*

"I'd be happy to carry your suitcase," he repeated, as he helped her to her feet.

"Thank you, Eugene. I *am* tired, and I appreciate your generosity."

"It's my pleasure." He picked up her suitcase, while she grabbed her overnight bag and purse. He held his arm out for her to take as he walked her across the street.

"I can see that chivalry is alive and well in

Franklin, Kentucky," said Cecilia, and she laughed for the first time in months.

"We aim to please, Cecilia." He led her to one of the double glass doors of the hotel and opened it.

She stepped in and looked around. The interior was as amazing as the exterior. *Elegant: that's the word.* No boring carpeting, but highly polished checkered squares of black and white marble flooring, and the two stories high lobby's focal point containing a horseshoe shaped curved staircase leading to the second floor. The cherry banister, wrapped in holly and cranberries was another splendid part of the stylish lobby. *I can't wait to explore this amazing hotel. The Woodsons certainly did not exaggerate their opinion of Christmas Hotel.*

In the middle of the horseshoe of the staircase stood a life-size model of the manger scene, and Mary, Joseph, the shepherd men, all watching the small babe in the manger. The life-size barn animals surrounded the lovely scene.

A Christmas tree in the middle of the room nearly touched the ceiling to the second floor. As Cecilia reveled in the magnificence of the tree and the beautiful ornaments and twinkling lights, she lifted her chin and saw the lovely angel atop the tree, smiling down on her in greeting. Several sofas, high back chairs, and cherry end tables decorated the room, with beautiful oriental rugs in the middle of the furniture groupings. A fire roared in a massive stone fireplace. She walked forward to examine the fireplace mantle shelf where six stockings hung, with names for Christopher, Jerilyn, Ken, Carrie Emeline, Lydia Grace, and Chris on one side, and on the other side two stockings for Lily and John, whose stockings were each the same size as the other six, along with four small stockings: Brian, Teresa, Mary Beth, and Ellie.

Along the wall off to the side of the room, behind a long lobby desk, she noticed for the first time a handsome middle-age couple sitting on high stools, watching her while she surveyed the room. Slightly embarrassed from staring, she turned and walked toward them. Eugene followed.

"Hello, Eugene," said the man. "I see you brought us a guest."

"Well, sir, I actually found her a few doors down and across the street, sitting on a park bench." He looked down at Cecilia and smiled. "She appeared to be a damsel in distress, but then I discovered she was just travel weary. Miss Cecilia Edmondson, I leave you in the capable hands of your hosts, Mr. and Mrs. Wright. Enjoy your stay." He made a mock bow, and she laughed.

She curtsied to him and said, "Thank you again,

Mr. Scott, for your chivalry." At that, Eugene took his leave.

She turned back to the Wrights. Mr. Wright made the introductions. "Miss Edmonson, we are pleased to meet you." He placed his arm around the woman. "This lovely lady is my wife Jerilyn, and I am Christopher. We are the proprietors of Christmas Hotel."

He and his wife extended their hands, and Cecilia shook hands with both of them. She noticed the friendly smiles on each face. The smiles appeared genuine, and Cecilia began to relax. *I'm liking this town more and more.*

"I have a letter of introduction from a couple who stayed here on their honeymoon twenty years ago." Cecilia handed the letter to Mr. Wright, and he held it so his wife could also read. Cecilia examined their faces as they read. She held her breath, and hoped she would not see pity.

She saw no sign of pity, and exhaled in relief as Mr. Wright folded the letter and returned it to the envelope, along with the check. He turned, removed the key on the wall for room number eight, and handed it to her.

Jerilyn smiled and nodded. "This is quite sufficient, Miss Edmondson. Breakfast is every morning at six o'clock. We have a meal at noon, and supper is every evening at six o'clock," and she pointed in the direction of the dining room. "We would like for you to join us for the evening meal at our table in the dining room at six o'clock on Friday. Two of our children will be joining us. They like to meet the new guests, especially the young ones who are alone."

"Thank you for the offer," said Cecilia. "I'm tired, and I'm not sure I'll be able. I want to spend my time resting."

"Whatever you decide, I hope you'll enjoy your stay at Christmas Hotel," said Christopher. "I will escort you to your room." At that, he stepped from around the desk, picked up her suitcase, and led her up the staircase.

Chapter Eight

Changes

*"Peace I leave with you, my peace I give unto you:
not as the world giveth, give I unto you. Let not
your heart be troubled, neither let it be afraid."*
John 14:27

Tuesday, December 12, 1967
Gloria Reynolds drove away from Gary, Indiana, just after daybreak. It was a pleasant day for a drive. The sun shined, the temperature steady around twenty-five degrees, thankfully with no snow. Her parents gave her their blessing, and they appeared to have no qualms about her leaving. In fact, they even encouraged her. She expected some reservations, but they showed none.

With no further news from the United States War Department, she could see little point in remaining any longer for news. Her parents acquired the phone number for Christmas Hotel and they could reach her there if they learned anything about Matthew. Anyway, it was unlikely that there would be more information from the army for several weeks. Maybe never. Some soldiers just disappeared for ever, MIA.

Her two-year-old secondhand 1965 deep blue Mustang convertible had been a graduation gift from her parents, and she made the seven hour drive with no difficulties. She stopped one time in Elizabethtown, Kentucky to refuel, and have lunch at the Shoney's Restaurant.

Gloria arrived in Franklin, Kentucky around three o'clock in the afternoon. She drove around the small town to check out the sites. On South College Street she located the high school. According to a sign out front, a new high school had been built behind the old one, and students were leaving the new campus, rushing in all directions.

She drove further along South College Street and turned right on West Cedar Street. Gloria drove slowly, surveying the businesses around the square and the courthouse within the square. The courthouse, light poles, and the trees in the park-like setting were decorated. Downtown Franklin was definitely quaint and charming, just as her parents described.

On the south side of the square, Lerman Brothers Department Store was probably the most dressed up for Christmas, with a mechanical Santa Claus and his reindeer moving quite life-like in the windows, and artificial snow falling from the ceiling. In the background, Santa's mechanical elves "fashioned" popular toys and gifts for sale: G.I. Joe figures, Chatty Kathy Dolls, ice skates, sleds, and red wagons. The display beckoned customers to stop in and purchase gifts.

On the west side of the square, the First Methodist Church of Franklin and the Franklin Presbyterian Church each displayed Nativity scenes out front along with signs announcing the hours of worship. Also, on the same side, the Franklin Flower Shop window exhibited a beautifully arranged array of potted Poinsettia plants, table centerpieces, and wreaths.

On the east side, at the corner of East Cedar and North Main, Christmas Hotel definitely stood out. Gloria parked the Mustang and stared. What a beautiful old Italianate structure. No wonder her parents and Matthew's parents still spoke about it today.

She stepped out of the car and inhaled the fresh clean air. Born and raised in Gary, Indiana, a town with a population of around 175,000, and known for its steel mills, Franklin, Kentucky, was a pleasant respite from her hometown. The air smelled fresh in this small town of approximately 6,000 people, according to the sign when she entered the town, unlike the harsh odors emitted from Gary's steel mills. More good news: her eyes no longer stung from the irritants in the air, so she'd not need eye drops when she walked outside. She meandered around the square, and people smiled, nodded to her, many said "Hi". No one appeared to be in the hurry she was accustomed to seeing in Gary.

At the very least, a Christmas wreath adorned the front door of all the businesses. She knew why her parents fell in love with Franklin. She, also, was rapidly falling in love with this picturesque beauty that resembled a Norman Rockwell painting.

"Matthew would like this," she said out loud.

She walked back to her car and started the motor. She just sat in silence. She was in no rush. "Your Precious Love" came on her car's radio station, sung by Marvin Gaye and Tammi Terrell. Gloria hung her head in remembrance. She and Matthew had danced to this song at their senior prom. She sat and listened to the whole song. "Oh, Matthew, we have had so much history together in our eighteen short years. I think that any song that comes on the radio will always remind me of you."

Tears streamed down her face. She looked up, and through blurred vision she watched a smiling happy young couple holding hands stroll past her car.

She grabbed some tissues from her purse, blew her nose and wiped her tears. Then looking into her visor mirror she checked her makeup. Needing to repair the damage, Cecelia hunted through her purse and found her powder compact. Finally, with her make-up patched up as well as possible, she opened the car door and again stepped out. Purse clutched in one hand, she retrieved her suitcase from the back seat with the other, and walked across the street to Christmas Hotel.

She opened one of the heavy double doors, crossed the threshold, and was immediately overwhelmed by the magnificence of the lobby, as surely many others had before her. The marble floor, a grand horseshoe shaped staircase, a life-size Nativity scene, the two-story high Christmas tree, all dressed in exquisite grandeur. A man and woman sat on high stools behind the check-in desk and stood to greet her. They smiled, and Gloria could not help but return the gesture.

"Welcome to Christmas Hotel. My name is Christopher Wright and this is my wife Jerilyn. We are the owners of Christmas Hotel."

They held out their hands, and she set down her suitcase and shook each hand. "My name is Gloria Reynolds. I would like to stay for a week or so. I hope you have a room. My parents stayed here in nineteen forty-six on a joint honeymoon with another couple. They have told me many wonderful stories about Christmas Hotel and this town. Do you have a room available?"

She became aware of a recognizable concern in her voice and knew she was rambling. It crossed her mind that since she had not made a reservation, there might not be a room for her.

"We are pleased to have you choose to stay with us," said Christopher. "Do not be alarmed, Miss Reynolds. We have a room for you. Are you by yourself?"

"Yes, sir, it will just be for me."

"We can give you room number nine. In fact, you will be right beside another young lady around your age. Maybe you'll meet and become friends." Mr. Wright presented a genuine smile as he handed over the key.

Gloria was not sure she wanted to get chummy with another girl. She wanted peace and quiet, and a change of scenery. She was definitely not here to socialize.

"Maybe," she replied, but she knew in her heart, "probably not" would have been more accurate, although a ruder response.

Jerilyn explained the times for the three meals. "On Friday evening we'll have dinner in the dining room at six o'clock." Jerilyn pointed in the direction. "Please join Mr. Wright and me at our family table. Two of our children will be with us. It will be our way of welcoming you to Christmas Hotel."

Gloria glanced from one smiling face to the other. These people were friendly, but she didn't want to get too friendly with them. "Thanks for the offer." Then, "Maybe," she added.

"Well, whatever you need, please ask," offered Christopher pleasantly. He walked around the desk and picked up her suitcase. "Please follow me, and you can get settled in your room."

Gloria followed Christopher up the staircase. *Well, I'm committed now. No turning around.*

Chapter Nine

Change of Scenery

*"I am feeble and sore broken: I have roared by
reason of the disquietness of my heart."*
Psalms 38:8

Friday morning, December 15, 1967
Loretta and Lydia Grace loaded the last bag into the
trunk of Lydia Grace's little 1967 red Corvair with
the white convertible top and a spotless white
leather interior. Loretta had never seen a car with
the trunk in the front and the engine in the rear,
and in a moment of loathing she realized the car
looked so much like Lydia Grace: clean and pure.

Lydia Grace slid into the driver's seat. Loretta
sat beside her and closed her passenger side door.
As she shifted the car into reverse via a small tab on
the dashboard, she spoke a warning to Loretta.
"The drive will be around four hours. By the time
we stop for lunch and refuel, we should arrive in
Franklin by two o'clock. But to pass the time, I
brought some 8-track tapes, and all with Christmas
songs. They're in the glove compartment. Would

you like to play one?"

"Sure." Loretta opened the glove box, selected a tape, and inserted it in the 8-track player. Although Loretta was not looking forward to this Christmas vacation, it was a better scenario than staying back at the college, and possibly encountering Barry and/or his frat brothers. She shuddered at the thought.

Lydia Grace evidently saw the shudder. "Are you okay?" she asked in her sweet voice with genuine concern.

At one time, Loretta liked people like Lydia Grace, and she herself had been somewhat like her. However, since the car accident that killed her parents, and the frat party, she found people like Lydia Grace rather nauseating. However, she did her best to disguise her feelings. After all, Lydia Grace and her family were doing her a huge favor. She certainly didn't have the money to go away on her own. Eventually, there would be a settlement from her parents' estate, but the attorney said it might take a while. In the meantime, she needed to be frugal. Her mother would tell her to be polite and act like a lady. She merely responded to Lydia Grace and said. "Yes, I'm fine. Maybe a little chilly."

"Oh, I'll turn up the heat." Lydia Grace fiddled with the temperature control gauge.

"I'll do it for you, so you can keep your eyes on

the road." Lydia Grace shot her a grateful smile.

I hope she doesn't think we'll become best friends during this vacation, because that will not happen.

They arrived at the Elizabethtown, Kentucky, exit off Interstate-65 South, and drove straight to the gas station. "At least the gas is only thirty-three cents a gallon here," remarked Lydia Grace. "In Cincinnati it's thirty-five cents a gallon. Highway robbery," but she laughed.

While the attendant gassed the car, washed the windshield, and checked the oil, the girls visited the ladies room. When they returned, the smiling attendant reported that the oil was fine. "That will be three dollars and thirty cents for the gas, Miss."

Lydia Grace counted out the money. "Thank you, sir." She turned to Loretta. "There's a Shoney's Restaurant across the street. Will that be okay with you for our lunch?"

"I don't know what a Shoney's Restaurant is," responded Loretta.

Lydia Grace thought for a second. "Think of it as a Frisch's Big Boy in the North."

"That's fine."

After finishing their lunch of hamburgers, french fries, and chocolate shakes, they continued on their drive and arrived in Franklin in under two hours.*

****

Lydia Grace exited Interstate-65 and drove into downtown Franklin. Loretta gaped out the window at the historic old homes they passed, and Lydia Grace wondered what her roommate was thinking. Within minutes they were in the center of the small town with the square and a courthouse in the middle of the park-like setting, with businesses all around.

Lydia Grace parked the car. "We're here!"

They each grabbed their purses and closed the car doors behind them. Loretta stopped for a moment and scrutinized the exterior of the hotel. Although Loretta said nothing, she presented the same look of awe that all visitors beheld when they first saw Christmas Hotel. Lydia Grace walked to the front of the Corvair, and used her trunk key to open it. Loretta would be staying at Christmas Hotel, and she retrieved Loretta's suitcase and closed the hood then set the suitcase on the sidewalk. She left her own suitcase in the trunk, as she would be going to her home on South College Street with her family.

Loretta finished her assessment of the building, picked up her suitcase, and together they walked up to the double glass doors. Since it was Friday, Charles the doorman was on duty for the weekend. Lydia Grace had never known a weekend without Charles, who had been the doorman for the past twenty years.

He held the massive door for them. "Welcome home, Miss Lydia Grace. It's good to see you."

"It's good to see you, too, Mr. Charles. I'd like for you to meet my roommate and friend Loretta Jenkins from the University of Cincinnati. She'll be staying with us at Christmas Hotel for the Christmas vacation."

"I welcome you, too, Miss Loretta. I hope you'll enjoy your stay." His wonderful smile spread nearly from ear to ear. "I'll take your suitcase, Miss Loretta."

When the girls stepped over the threshold, Charles carried the suitcase to the front desk, while Loretta ran her eyes around the interior. Lydia Grace rushed to her parents who left their stools from behind the long cherry desk and hurried to Lydia Grace. They hugged and kissed, and the questions began.

"How was your trip, honey?" asked her mother.

"Actually, it was a very pleasant drive. Thankfully, we didn't encounter any snow or rain, and there were no accidents along the way."

"Did you stop in Elizabethtown for lunch?" asked her father.

"Most definitely! It's a good stopping place for the drive down, and at about the halfway mark. I gassed there, too, and the price was two cents cheaper than in Cincinnati. The Corvair doesn't eat much gas, though. It was a wonderful high school graduation gift from you both." She smiled at each parent. "I still could not be happier with my little car, and I'm taking good care of it."

"I'm sure you are," nodded her father. "I think I've drummed into you the importance of good maintenance."

"Yes, Daddy, you have." She nodded back with a wink and a grin.

"Is this your friend and roommate Loretta you told us about?" asked her mother.

Loretta stood by the Christmas tree, inspecting the manger scene, fireplace, and the horseshoe-shaped cherry staircase.

"Yes, she is." Lydia Grace frowned. "Sadly she doesn't say much," she added in a whisper. "As I wrote you, her parents died not too long ago, but I think there may be something else bothering her. She's not the same sweet girl she was last summer."

They watched Loretta as she continued to survey the majesty of the lobby of Christmas Hotel. Lydia Grace turned back to her parents and saw the small smile on her mother's face as she watched Loretta. Her mother had arrived here years ago, and told the story many times of her first impression of Christmas Hotel. She enjoyed reliving that first "wow moment" as she described it, through each new guest.

Finally, Loretta turned around.

"Hello, Loretta, and welcome to Christmas Hotel," said Lydia Grace's father, as he strode toward Loretta and shook her hand.

Lydia Grace and her mom walked up beside him.

"Welcome to Christmas Hotel! I'm Jerilyn Wright and my husband is Christopher," and she also shook Loretta's hand. "We've booked you in room number ten, near two other young ladies. However, as a friend of Lydia Grace, you are also welcome to stay at our home a couple of blocks away, if you would rather."

"Thank you for the offer of your home, Mrs. Wright, but presently I would prefer to stay at Christmas Hotel. That is, if you don't mind."

"Whatever you feel is better for you, Loretta. Maybe you and the two other young ladies who have checked in all alone this Christmas season will meet and become friends."

"We'll see."

"In the meantime, I'll escort you to your room so you can get settled," said Christopher, while handing her the key to room #10. "Dinner is at six o'clock. Lydia Grace and our twelve-year-old son Chris will both be here. You're invited to join us at our table, as our welcome to Christmas Hotel."

"Thank you, sir, and I'll consider your invitation." Loretta said goodbye for now to Lydia Grace, and followed Christopher up the steps to room number ten.

Chapter Ten

Revelations

"The Lord is nigh unto them that are of a broken heart; and saveth such as be of a contrite spirit."
Psalms 34:18

Friday Evening at Dinner, December 15, 1967
When Christopher and Jerilyn entered the dining room, they added an extra table and three more chairs in anticipation that Cecilia, Gloria, and Loretta would accept their invitation for dinner.

They sat around their family table by the french doors that led to the interior courtyard with Lydia Grace and Chris. This particular space, long considered the best view of the dining room and courtyard had been used by the original owners Thomas and Lucy Hoy, and later for Captain and Mrs. Bazell, the second owners.

Christopher looked at his watch and said aloud, "It's a minute past six o'clock. It doesn't appear they're coming."

"Patience, darling," said Jerilyn with a smile,

patting his arm.

Lydia Grace glanced toward the door. "There's Loretta!" She smiled and waved Loretta to the table.

Christopher and Chris stood. "Thank you for coming," said Christopher, as their son Chris held the chair for Loretta, seating her beside Lydia Grace.

A minute later, Jerilyn observed Cecilia and Gloria standing in the doorway, looking around and confused. The girls spotted Christopher and Jerilyn, and they made their way slowly toward the table. Both girls viewed the other, a bit guarded, since neither had met. Christopher and Chris were still standing, and each of them held a chair to seat Cecilia and Gloria.

"Welcome to dinner at Christmas Hotel," Jerilyn said to all of the young ladies. "For those of you that don't know our children, I'll introduce you. Loretta, you already know our daughter Lydia Grace, and this is our son Chris."

Loretta and Chris nodded one to the other. "Cecilia and Gloria, you don't know Lydia Grace or Chris, but I hope our children, Loretta, and you two will all become friends during your stay at Christmas Hotel."

Cecilia, Gloria and Loretta nodded and returned the obligatory smiles.

"I second Jerilyn's hope," said Christopher. "In fact we can get started now. Lydia Grace and Chris, why don't you two share something about yourselves, and then Cecilia, Gloria, and Loretta can do the same. Actually, on second thoughts, I think I'll go first and then Jerilyn can share.

He didn't miss a beat, but continued by saying, "My full name is Christopher Joseph Wright, and I was born and raised in Franklin, Kentucky. I may sound a little prejudiced, but I think you're going to meet here in Franklin, and *all* of Simpson County, Kentucky, some of the kindest, giving, and genuinely sincere people you have ever come across. Our oldest daughter Lily is married, and lives near here with her husband John and their four children in Russellville, Kentucky. She's a high school English and French teacher in Russellville. Her husband is the high school physical education and the general science teacher. It's hard to believe, but Lily is now thirty-one years old!"

He was interrupted by the waiter asking for their order.

Christopher addressed Cecilia, Gloria, and Loretta. "Ladies, the four of us have decided on the special, which is roast beef, mashed potatoes and gravy, green beans, fried squash, coleslaw, and southern cornbread. We highly recommend it, unless you'd prefer something different."

The girls all nodded and said that the special would be fine. The waiter returned to the kitchen and then Jerilyn began.

"Christopher was born and raised here, but I arrived in December of nineteen forty-one from Dayton, Ohio. I met Christopher and later his daughter Lily, and over a very short period of time fell in love with both of them. Christopher and I were married in the chapel here at Christmas Hotel on New Year's Eve, nineteen forty-one. In nineteen forty-two, not only Kenneth Elliot Wright was born, but his two-minute younger twin Carrie Emeline Wright. I also find it hard to believe the ages of our children, but the twins are now twenty-five years old! Ken teaches algebra and geometry at the University of Kentucky, along with working on his masters in biology. He'll be home tomorrow for Christmas break, and you can meet him, too. Carrie Emeline is also a teacher. She teaches second grade at the elementary school in Bowling Green, Kentucky. We also expect her home tomorrow to spend time with us until she returns to school early in January."

Lydia Grace and Chris sat across from Jerilyn, and she continued. "We were then blessed with Lydia Grace in nineteen forty-six and Chris in nineteen fifty-five," she said, while smiling at her children. "In fact, I do believe Lydia Grace has a

79

birthday coming up on Christmas Eve," she added with a wink and a lift of one eyebrow and a grin. She looked directly at Lydia Grace. "Usually, by now, you've hinted about what you want for your birthday present *and* Christmas present, but we haven't heard a word this year."

Lydia Grace simply responded in the same playful manner as her mom, and said, "I'll let you surprise me this year."

Jerilyn looked over at Cecilia, Gloria, and Loretta. "Lydia Grace insists we wrap her birthday presents in white, and her Christmas presents in Christmas wrap, and place them all under the tree. That way, she doesn't feel we've combined the two celebrations.

"Tomorrow, we'll drive out to the McLemore farm, as we do each year to cut down the Christmas tree for our home on South College Street. It's been a joint family tradition: the Wrights and the McLemores, since the Christmas of nineteen forty-two. Lily, her husband John, and their four children will arrive later this evening for the tree cutting tomorrow. They take a tree back to their home in Russellville, after helping all of us decorate our own tree – along with the outside decorations at our home. You three young ladies are welcome to join us for the tree cutting. We'll gather in the lobby, and leave from Christmas Hotel tomorrow morning at nine o'clock."

Lydia Grace added, "If you decide to come, wear warm clothes and boots. If it snows, you'll need the boots. Keep in mind we'll be on a farm. There are other things to step in."

Jerilyn chuckled as she saw the look of revulsion on their faces. *These three young ladies are obviously born-and-bred city girls. They've probably never set foot on a working farm.*

The dinners arrived and it was Lydia Grace's turn to share. Between bites she began. "I'm Lydia Grace Wright, as it was pointed out. I room with Loretta at the University of Cincinnati, but I attend UC for the Conservatory of Music, and I'm on a music scholarship. Thanks to my father's piano lessons since I was eight years old, I've been engrossed in music: classical in particular. I suppose it's a generational thing. My father's mother taught piano here in Franklin. I hope to become a concert pianist and write more compositions. To date, I've written seven compositions, and three are published. I also play several other instruments." She turned to Chris. "That's all. It's your turn, little brother."

"I'm Christopher Joseph Wright, Jr., but everyone calls me Chris, I suppose to differentiate me from my father who is called Christopher. I'm in seventh grade, and our seventh and eighth grade class moved into the old Franklin High School building this past September. As my parents already told you, my three oldest siblings became teachers. Lydia Grace will be a wonderful composer and concert pianist, but I want to follow my parents in the management of Christmas Hotel. I love working here at our hotel, and I can't think of anywhere else I'd rather be."

He waved his hand around the dining room. "When I'm not in school, the chefs are teaching me their skills, and I'm learning about managing the dining room from the former dining room hostess – who happens to be my mother." He looked at Jerilyn and smiled. "I'm learning front desk management from my father and Mr. Mullins his assistant manager. I'm even learning about cleaning and supplying the guest rooms, from the cleaning staff. I realize that no job is unimportant. Every position at Christmas Hotel must be performed to the best of one's ability. My parents have instilled that work ethic in me; in fact in all of their children. I hope that someday I can be the one to continue the mission of Christmas Hotel, that Christ's birth should be celebrated daily. I thank my parents for raising me in their beliefs."

"Thank you, Chris," said Christopher, with a slight hoarseness in his voice. "Cecilia, would you like to share next?"

She took a bite, finished chewing, and wiped her mouth. "I'm not good at this," she said bluntly. "You know ... speaking in public ... especially about myself. I'm from Houston, Texas. I have wonderful parents and two little brothers. I graduated from high school on June fourth this year. The main story of my life is between June fifth this year and today, but I'm not comfortable sharing that information. I'm sorry." She hung her head.

"It's okay, Cecilia," said Jerilyn with understanding. "If at any time you wish to talk, Christopher and I are here or on call twenty-four hours a day. The chapel is also open around the clock if you'd like to pray."

"Thank you," was all Cecilia could muster.

"Gloria, will you tell us about yourself?" asked Jerilyn.

Gloria paused so long that Jerilyn didn't think she would share either. Finally she said, "I graduated high school on June fourth this year, too, and I'm from Gary, Indiana. My father is a deacon in our church, and my fiancé's father is the pastor. In fact, our parents stayed here at Christmas Hotel in nineteen forty-six for a joint honeymoon."

"That's amazing!" interrupted Cecilia, turning to look at Gloria in surprise. "My benefactors, who arranged for me to stay here, honeymooned at Christmas Hotel in nineteen forty-seven. What a coincidence!"

Gloria returned Cecilia's statement with a smile. Jerilyn and Christopher shot each other that special knowing smile. "Gloria, who are your parents and your fiancé's parents?" asked Christopher. "A great many couples honeymoon here, but we may still remember them."

"My parents are Ralph and Irene Reynolds, and Matthew's parents are Pastor Warren Johnson and Bertha Johnson," said Gloria.

"I remember them!" said Jerilyn. "The men were both in the Second World War in Germany, but I believe they'd been friends before the war, too."

"That's true. They were friends since childhood, just like Matthew ... my fiancé ... and I have been. After they married, they purchased homes side by side. Matthew and I were born in nineteen forty-nine, just one day apart."

"Where is Matthew now?" Lydia Grace asked.

Gloria glanced down at her lap, but then returned Lydia Grace's gaze. "He's in Vietnam ... but I don't know where. He's been reported MIA." A tear slid down her cheek, and she quickly wiped it away.

Jerilyn stood and walked over to Gloria's chair. She placed her arm around Gloria. "If you ever want to discuss Matthew, Christopher and I are here. In fact, Christopher is a preacher, too. Although, he does not pastor a church, he preaches many Sundays here at Christmas Hotel." She hugged Gloria and patted her arm.

The hug brought more tears to Gloria's eyes, and she tried to hide them with her napkin. "Thank you, Mrs. Wright. I appreciate that, but at the moment I don't think I can continue to share." Her voice broke and quivered.

"That's understandable." She softly patted Gloria on the back and returned to her seat.

"Loretta, would you like to share now?" asked Jerilyn.

Like Cecilia and Gloria, it took Loretta a moment to answer. "As you already know, I share a room with Lydia Grace at the University of Cincinnati. We have three of our classes together: history, music, and English. I have one brother in the United States Air Force and he's currently stationed in Germany. His name is Donald and he's ten years older than I am, so I really don't know him that well." She stopped, and appeared to clam up.

Jerilyn studied her, and then said," Have you seen him lately?"

"I saw him a couple of months ago. He returned from Germany when my parents died in a car crash. He came home for the funeral, but couldn't stay long." Loretta shed no tears. Her features and words were almost robotic.

Jerilyn said softly, "I'm sorry for your loss, Loretta."

The other five murmured words of sympathy, too. It grew quiet at the table, but everyone had finished the dinner. The waiter came by for the dessert order. At first Cecilia, Gloria, and Loretta declined, but the waiter did not give up. He enticed them with the chef's fresh-from-the-oven apple cobbler, with a scoop of vanilla ice cream on top.

As soon as they finished the dessert, Cecilia, Gloria, and Loretta thanked the Wrights for dinner, but excused themselves to retire to their rooms. Before they left, Jerilyn reminded them of the tree cutting the next day.

"Do you think they'll show up in the morning?" Jerilyn asked Christopher.

"I don't know, honey. I think that all three of them are troubled young ladies. I don't know what to make of them. We'll have to pray about how to help each one."

"I do know that Loretta used to be much different," offered Lydia Grace. "Up until the car crash, she was practically the nicest girl on campus. Something changed in her personality shortly after the death of her parents, and she's gradually become more distraught. I try to be her friend, but

I'll admit sometimes it's really hard. She can be outright hostile, but I know deep down that's not the real Loretta. I know she's in pain. I know she misses her parents, but quite often I think it's more than that, and I can't put my finger on it."

"We'll pray for all of them," said Christopher, checking his watch. "In the meantime, we need to hurry home. I imagine we may have children and grandchildren waiting for us at home."

Chapter Eleven

Cecilia

"Lover and friend hast thou put far from me,
and mine acquaintance into darkness."
Psalms 88; 18

Friday Evening after Dinner, December 15, 1967
Cecilia entered room number eight, locked the door, and tossed her room key onto the desk. Her stomach still mildly ached where the baby had been cut from her womb. It was a constant reminder of what she had done. It was only the memory of Mr. Woodson the taxi driver and his family that made life even a little bit bearable, but there was pain – both physical and mental.

She walked over to the television, pulled the power knob and turned the channel to CBS. While waiting to make sure the television was completely warmed up, she opened the drapes, and then adjusted the rabbit ears to get the best reception before plopping down on the bed. On Friday evenings, she had always enjoyed Robert Conrad in "The Wild Wild West" and "Gomer Pyle U.S.M.C."

that followed. Actually, those were the shows she watched on Friday evening with her family before leaving with Ernie last summer.

Tonight, she was unable to concentrate on either program. Her thoughts kept drifting to last summer, and Ernie and her high school graduation day. On June fourth, she and her family had a quick lunch, attended the church service, and afterwards the graduation service.

As soon as the ceremony was over, she had hurried to the ladies room where she had stashed her jeans, a summer shirt, socks, and tennis shoes in a locker. She changed and handed the cap, gown, dress, and dress shoes to her mother. She said she was meeting Ernie; and was gone before her parents could ask questions. She didn't tell them where she was going. She had left her parents a short note in her room to be found after she was gone. She'd let them find the note. When she rode off with Ernie, she thought it would be a wonderful adventure. She wanted freedom from her parents, church, and school. She had helped Ernie pack the saddlebags of his 1960 Harley-Davidson motorcycle the night before, so that she would not need to return home after the graduation ceremony.

Cecilia and Ernie rode the two thousand mile trip in three days and two nights. They camped in parks along the way. When they entered the

Haight-Ashbury neighborhood of San Francisco, a flood of young people walked around; many barefoot. If they wore anything on their feet, it was usually sandals or moccasins. Some did wear gym shoes. The women had on brightly colored, flowered dresses and many had flowers in their hair. Some had young children in tow, but all of them, male or female, sported long hair with decorative headbands. They strolled the streets of the old neighborhood openly smoking marijuana or hashish. She and Ernie rode by the street musicians, as well as the pan handlers who walked uptown for the rich to drop money in the pan.

The Haight-Ashbury neighborhood was old-fashioned, and probably beautiful in its heyday, but now it was run down. However, this was just the adventure they were looking for. Ernie parked the bike and removed the key before they hopped off. Cecilia didn't remember a time when her backside hurt more. She was nervous, but very excited. At least she had Ernie with her.

They walked up to a young couple leaning against the side of a building, listening to the psychedelic music from the street musicians. Ernie spoke to them first. "Hi. My name is Ernie and this here's my woman Cecilia," he said, hugging Cecilia close. "We just arrived, and are wondering if you can tell us where we can crash."

The young man said nothing; only pointed to a vacancy sign in a fourth floor window across the street, then turned back to watch the musicians. Cecilia noticed the vacant stare. Clearly, the young man and woman were both stoned.

Cecilia and Ernie rented the one-room apartment with a small kitchen alcove. The whole building had been cut up into tiny apartments, as with other houses in the neighborhood. Obviously, the slum landlords were trying to jam as many people as possible into their buildings. None of the tenants locked their doors. People could wander into anyone's apartment night or day, and often did.

Within a few days, Cecilia and Ernie fit right in. The drugs were plentiful, and they now knew what living in a commune would be like. They met new music groups like Jefferson Airplane, the Grateful Dead, and Janis Joplin, who all lived a short distance from the intersection of Haight and Ashbury. The groups tried out many of their songs on the hippies – as they were called – before the songs were later recorded. A local theatre company passed out free food every afternoon at 4:00.

The hippies and their children lined up for the food and sat anywhere they pleased. They had taken over the neighborhood. Most came for the freedom from parental supervision, but many came for the liberal politics of the day and were brainwashed into an extreme radical belief.

Ernie displayed a different side to him that Cecilia never saw back in Houston. He was hot-tempered and verbally and physically abusive, except when he was stoned. She confronted him when she caught him flirting with a girl down the hall. Ernie slapped her and told her to mind her own business.

He stepped into the room where the girl lived, and slammed the door in Cecilia's face. "Stay out!" he shouted to her.

Cecilia was crushed, but slunk back to their room in defeat. Ernie didn't come back for two days, and when he did, he was stoned. He said he was sorry, and it wouldn't happen again. It did though, and many times that summer. By late September Cecilia was ready to leave. The great adventure had turned sour. Many had already left the neighborhood; mostly college students returning to their schools.

On October 6, 1967, those remaining in the Haight staged a mock funeral, "The Death of the Hippie" ceremony, to signify the end of an era. The message of the mock funeral was explained as follows: "We want to signal that this is the end of it. Don't come back here. Stay where you are! Take the revolution to where you live. Don't come back, because it's over and done with."

Cecilia now realized that the whole "summer of love" was politically motivated.

She walked away from Ernie. She refused to ride back home with him. He rode away and she later hitched a ride with another couple heading to Chicago. They left her in Omaha, Nebraska. From there she hitched a ride to Dallas, and then another ride to her friend Donna's apartment in Houston.

"No, I don't miss Ernie, and I don't miss last summer," she said aloud. She jumped up, turned off the television, and closed the drapes. After changing into her pajamas, she slipped under the bed covers, turned out the light, and fell into a restless sleep.

Chapter Twelve

Gloria

*"Blessed are they that mourn: for they
shall be comforted."*
Matthew 5:4

Friday Evening after Dinner, December 15, 1967
Gloria returned to room number nine, threw her
room key on the desk, and switched on her radio.
"Never My Love" by The Association played. The
first stanza asked if there was a time when I'd grow
tired of you.

"Oh, Matthew," she said aloud and sighed, "I
could never grow tired of you. I have loved you
since we were babies." She threw herself onto the
bed and cried into her pillow as she listened to the
song.

The next stanza asked if her heart would lose its
desire for him.

"I will never lose my desire for you, Matthew. I
love you so much. Are you alive?"

The third stanza said that a love would not end,
and she agreed that her life depended on Matthew.

"All I can think of is you, Matthew. My life *does* depend on you. I don't want to live without you," she said aloud as she cupped her stomach, which was still flat. "In another month or two this baby is going to show. What do I do, Matthew? Do I keep the baby? Give it up for adoption? Abort it? I need you, Matthew." She continued to weep.

She spoke to Matthew as if he was there in the room with her. "That last evening, before you flew out the next morning, we said our vows to each other, and we asked God to be there with us. We said we'd love each other forever, and that nothing could separate us. We asked God to bless our union. Are we common-law married? We said we were, but we haven't told anyone. Does that negate our vows? Did God honor our marriage? Was our union a sin? If I give birth to this baby, will he or she be born in sin? I'm scared, Matthew. I don't know what to do. I need to talk to you. I need you to come home to me."

She began to cry loudly, and she turned the radio louder so she wouldn't be heard by Cecilia and Loretta in the rooms beside her. More songs played to remind her of Matthew.

"I should write my parents. I know they love me and worry about me. I wish you were here with me, Matthew. I'm in a beautiful hotel, owned and managed by a Christian family. Our parents honeymooned here. I wish we were here together right now and on our honeymoon. I wish you weren't MIA in Vietnam. I need you. I can't live without you. Please be okay, Matthew. I need to know what to do. If you're praying somewhere in Vietnam, please pray for us."

The last song she heard before falling asleep was Neil Diamond's "Thank the Lord for the Night Time". She did thank Him for the night time. It was only at night she could be alone and dwell on memories of Matthew.

Chapter Thirteen

Loretta

*"My days are like a shadow that declineth;
and I am withered like grass."*
Psalms 102:11

Friday Evening after Dinner, December 15, 1967
Loretta Jenkins crossed the threshold into room number ten, closed the door, and set the locks. For just a moment she leaned against the door and closed her eyes. Her thoughts began to ramble.

These are good people, but I don't belong here. I used to think of myself as a good person. Now, I've just become bitter. Why me? What did I do to deserve all this? Why did my parents die in that car crash? They were good people and too young to die. I can't believe I went to that party to spend time with Barry. Deep down, I knew he was no good. I'm so dumb and naïve. Did I really think he'd be different with me when he invited me upstairs? Or when it happened, did I think I somehow deserved it?

I wish my mom was here. I need someone to talk to. I need help. This disgusting situation with a fetus growing inside of me is driving me nuts. I suppose I could talk to Lydia Grace. Wow, that was a stupid thought! Little Miss Goody Two-Shoes would be appalled if I told her. She's probably never had anything bad ever happen to her. She grew up in this beautiful hotel with this amazing family. What would she know about heartbreak, pain, sorrow, and loneliness? What would she know about having nobody to love her? What would she know about depression? Lydia Grace was born with a silver spoon in her mouth.

Loretta pushed away from the door, walked to the window, and opened the drapes. She was given one of the rooms with windows overlooking the town square. It was indeed a lovely town. The businesses around the square and the square itself were beautifully decorated for Christmas. Couples sat on the benches, holding hands.

In the next block she saw on the marquis that *It's a Wonderful Life* was the movie currently playing at the Roxy Theater. The show must have just let out, because throngs of people walked from that direction. Everyone appeared to be having a good time on a pleasant Friday evening. *I hate that movie! It lets us think every life is important and how one life can affect other lives. I've had enough of those thoughts.* She closed the drapes in anger.

Christmas Hotel stationery lay on the desk in

her room. *Maybe I should write my brother, but what should I say? He's my only family, even if he barely knows me. I suppose I could tell him where I am and wish him a Merry Christmas.*

She sat down at the desk, picked up the pen, and began to write.

December 15, 1967

Dear Donald,
I'm on Christmas vacation from UC, and I thought I should write and let you know where I'm staying. My latest UC roommate Lydia Grace Wright invited me to her home in Franklin, Kentucky, for the holidays, and I have a room in the hotel her parents own. It's called Christmas Hotel, because they celebrate the birth of Christ year around. It's an elegant Italianate structure, built in 1850. This charming small town is quite lovely, and decorated for Christmas.

She paused and tapped the end of the pen against her chin. She thought about what she wrote; nearly wadding up the paper and throwing it away. *He's going to think I'm happy, and that I don't have a care in the world. Is that what I want him to believe? Yes, it is. He doesn't need to know*

I'm pregnant. If I abort this unwanted fetus, he'll never know. It can be just my secret. That's the best decision. I can go to my grave with no one knowing. She returned to the letter.

> *I'll be staying until New Year's Day. We have to be back on campus to resume classes on Tuesday, January second. I'm sorry I didn't get a package in the mail for you in time. That's something Mom always did, and I should have done that for you.*

She stopped again and thought about the last line. Without fail, her mom sent packages to Donald on his birthday and at Christmas. Maybe she could get her act together enough by his birthday to send a package. He always enjoyed treats, cassette music, and books from home; items he couldn't get in Germany.

> *I want you to know that I love you, and I wish you a Merry Christmas.*
> *Love,*
>
> *Loretta*

She found an envelope embossed with the Christmas Hotel logo and return address. She folded her letter, placed it in the envelope, and propped it upon the desk. Maybe the hotel could post it for her. Even though it would be sent air mail, she realized it might not arrive in time for Christmas.

She rose and prepared for bed. As she brushed her teeth, she thought about the Wright family's invitation to go to the farm tomorrow to cut down a tree. She brushed her hair, put on her pajamas, and slipped under the covers. Her last thoughts, when she turned off the lights, were that she had nothing else to do the next day, so she might as well go.

Chapter Fourteen

The McLemore Farm

*"A man that hath friends must shew himself
friendly: and there is a friend that sticketh
closer than a brother."*
Proverbs 18:24

Saturday Morning, December 16, 1967
It was a full house for the Wright Family, and
Christopher and Jerilyn could not be happier that
their five children, son-in-law, and four
grandchildren were all together and under the same
roof.

The five bedrooms were full again in the family
home at 210 South College Street. This had been
the home where Christopher grew up, only a few
blocks from Christmas Hotel. His parents bought
this historical home when they married in 1910. It
was known in Franklin as the Montague House,
built around 1860 by William Clement Montague.
Christopher and Jerilyn shared their master
bedroom, and Lily occupied her old room that she
now, of course, shared with her husband John
Demeter when they were in town. Ellie, their six-

month-old baby girl, slept in the cradle at the foot of their bed. The antique cradle had held and rocked four generations of Wright family babies.

Lydia Grace and Carrie Emeline continued to share their old room when they were home, and now Chris shared his room with Ken, which was formerly Ken's room anyway. They were joined by their nephew, six-year-old Brian. The room still held two sets of bunk beds. Five-year-old Teresa and three-year-old Mary Beth shared the double bed in the guest room.

The family assembled in the kitchen to cook the Saturday morning breakfast. As usual, Christopher and Jerilyn did most of the cooking, and their three daughters set the table. John, Ken, Chris, and even Lydia Grace's twelve-year-old German Shepherd Gabe entertained the four little ones.

As soon as breakfast was finished, Darius Scott, now the retired sheriff of Simpson County, his wife Barbara, and their two grown sons Eugene and William rang the doorbell. The Scott family made it a Christmas tradition to join the Wright family each year to cut down their own Christmas cedar tree at the McLemore farm. Darius and Barbara's two daughters Hazel and Sadie, along with Sadie's husband, Dr. Larry Isenhower, drove in from Nashville, and arrived within minutes after their parents and brothers. They would also be heading to the McLemore farm for the tree cutting.

"We need to stop first at Christmas Hotel," said Christopher. "There are three young ladies staying there, each by themselves, and Jerilyn and I invited them to go with us."

The Wright family along with Lydia Grace's dog Gabe, loaded into their 1966 Ford Econoline Van. Lily and John helped their four children into their 1965 Dodge Van. Darius, Barbara, Eugene, and William climbed into their 1966 Chrysler Town-and-Country Wagon. Sadie, Larry, and Hazel returned to Larry's 1965 Chevy Caprice.

****

All four vehicles parked along East Cedar Street, and Christopher, Jerilyn, Lydia Grace, Ken, and Eugene entered the hotel. Lydia Grace grinned with pleasure as she saw the three young ladies seated in the lobby on the sofas around the Christmas tree. The Wright family had hoped all three would join them.

Christopher made the car seating arrangements and said, "Cecilia, you can ride with Eugene and his family, and Loretta and Gloria can ride with my family." "Cecilia, I'm sure you'll remember Eugene from when you arrived in Franklin."

"Well, hello again, Miss Cecilia," said Eugene, smiling as he stepped out, took her hand and walked her to the car, seating her beside him.

"Hello, again to you, my chivalrous friend," said Cecilia looking up at him as she walked.

Lydia Grace moved over in the third seat of the Wrights' car, so that Gloria could sit with her and Carrie Emeline, and Ken directed Loretta to sit with Chris and him in the second seat. Gabe's large frame occupied the entire cargo department in the rear.

The four-vehicle caravan drove the twelve miles into the country, while a light snow began to fall. Christopher played Christmas music on his car's eight-track tape player.

Ken involved Loretta in conversation, and Ken's expressions appeared to be more than cordial attentiveness. Lydia Grace chuckled and nodded her approval to Carrie Emeline as Loretta responded likewise to Ken. Ken was describing his relationship with his older sister Lily. "She always teased me about shaking the gifts under the tree to guess what they held."

"My big brother Donald and I once unwrapped the presents before Christmas, and then we couldn't wrap them back exactly the same way. Of course we got in trouble – Donald primarily, because he was fourteen and I was only four."

Ken laughed and pointed back to Carrie Emeline. "My twin Carrie Emeline, who is chuckling in the backseat with my sister Lydia

Grace and I had once done the same thing around the age of seven."

Carrie Emeline smacked his pointed finger affectionately.

When Ken smiled at Loretta, Loretta returned the smile with a shy laugh.

Lydia Grace sat back, enjoying the friendly interaction between Ken and Loretta. *Maybe Ken can help Loretta this Christmas. If so, my prayers are being answered. Thank You Lord.*

The drivers parked the vehicles around the circular driveway at the McLemore farm, and car doors were opened and slammed closed. Gabe ran to play with the McLemore farm dogs and chase the barn cats. Booker and Nettie Sue stood on the front porch and waved a welcome. The snow began to fall harder. The visitors gathered into the nice warm kitchen and were greeted by Mama Harris, Nettie Sue's Mama, who was pouring steaming cups of hot chocolate, aided by Booker and Sue's fifteen-year-old son Robert. A picture of their nineteen-year-old son Jimmy in his army uniform hung prominently on the kitchen wall. Lydia Grace recently heard that Jimmy was now stationed in Vietnam.

After warming their bodies from the hot chocolate, everyone climbed onto Booker's hay wagon, and he pulled it with the tractor. They sang Christmas songs as the tractor carried them across the road to the second McLemore farm and over a bumpy hillside. Gabe and two of the McLemores' Treeing Walker Coonhound hunting dogs ran alongside the wagon, barking and playing in the snow that had already piled up.

Ken claimed a spot beside Loretta, and Eugene managed to squeeze in to sit beside Cecilia. Not wanting Gloria to feel left out, Lydia Grace crawled across a bale of hay to sit beside her. They had just finished singing "Rudolph the Red-Nosed Reindeer," when Booker stopped the tractor. They all jumped down, and Booker handed Robert, Ken, John, Larry, and Eugene the saws for the Christmas cedar trees. Each family gathered to pick out their favorite tree, sawed them down, and loaded them onto the center of the hay wagon. All the while, Christopher snapped pictures with his 1963 Canonflex RM camera with its large built-in light meter.

Lydia Grace could not think of an event that her father did not capture on film. There seemed to be hundreds of albums going clear back to his boyhood days, when he received his first camera in 1918 at the age of five from his own parents. It was an Eastman Kodak Brownie, which he still retained in his extensive camera collection.

The families and friends climbed back upon the wagon for the return trip across the road. Ken again managed to secure his seat beside Loretta, and Eugene sat beside Cecilia. Lydia Grace climbed on next to Gloria and off they went, the dogs again barking alongside the wagon; the coonhounds known for their friendly barking, encouraged old Gabe to bark louder.

Cecilia, Gloria, and Loretta were laughing when they arrived back at the farmhouse. "I've never been on a hayride before," said Loretta.

"Me either," said Cecilia.

"What fun." Gloria rubbed her backside. "I don't think the hay was very soft, though."

They all laughed, and Eugene said, "Well, you city girls just need to spend some time on a working farm."

"I'll have to think long and hard about that," Loretta responded with a chuckle and a rub to her backside also. The men tied their cedar trees to the tops of their vehicles, while Robert carried the McLemore tree into the farm house. The men thanked and shook hands with Booker, and the ladies hugged Nettie Sue. "We promise to attend Christopher's Candlelight Christmas Eve service in the chapel at Christmas Hotel," said Nettie Sue, as she waved goodbye to her friends.

*****

In previous years, when they arrived back at the Wright family home on South College Street, all of the Scott family returned to their own home to decorate their tree. However, this time Eugene said that he would hang around and help decorate with the Wrights. When Jerilyn smiled with the slight raise of her left eyebrow, Lydia Grace realized her mother, too, understood Eugene sought to spend the evening with Cecilia. The fact that her older brother Ken seemed smitten with Loretta had not gone unnoticed either. Jerilyn welcomed Eugene into their home, while the other men headed to the basement for the decorations and the tree stand.

As soon as the tree was righted, Jerilyn, Christopher, and Ken strung the tree lights. Lily placed little Ellie in the baby swing in the front parlor in view of the tree. "What do you think, Ellie?" asked Lily, and she cooed to her baby.

The baby laughed and jumped in her swing. This was baby Ellie's first Christmas. Lily laughed along with her. "She's going to be just as fascinated with all the decorations as her older sisters and brother" Lily kissed Ellie and said, "Mommy will be back soon."

Jerilyn smiled at her oldest daughter Lily. "Don't worry, Lily. I'll watch her for you."

Lily kissed Jerilyn on the cheek. "Thanks, Mom."

Lily, John, and their three older children bundled up and strung the outdoor lights on the balcony and above the front porch, while Chris and Eugene strung the lights around the front porch columns.

Cecilia, Gloria, and Loretta knelt down to baby Ellie and talked to her. The baby laughed and kicked her legs with excitement. The three girls laughed with the baby and clearly enjoyed Ellie's excitement. Lydia Grace watched the girls' interaction with the baby. *They seem to be coming out of their hard shells. They just needed to spend time with the Wright family. Please, Lord, keep helping them, and show my family and I how to help them this Christmas. I know something is troubling Loretta – and Cecilia and Gloria, too.*

When all the lights were strung around the house, Jerilyn handed boxes of ornaments and tinsel to everyone, while she and Christopher headed to the kitchen to make hot chocolate. Within the hour, the tree and house were decorated, and everyone crowded into the kitchen with Christopher and Jerilyn for a steaming mug.

"Let's all go into the living room," suggested Christopher. "Maybe we can entice our future concert pianist to play some Christmas songs, and we can sing along." He winked at Lydia Grace.

Lydia Grace returned the wink. "I'd love to, Daddy, if you'll sit beside me and play, too."

The young men carried in some of the dining

room chairs, so they all could sit together in the living room.

"Okay, what's the first request?" asked Lydia Grace.

Lily piped up, "You know my favorite is 'O Little Town of Bethlehem.'"

Lydia Grace and her dad chuckled. Ken poked his big sister, Lily and turned to Loretta on his other side, "We can't start any event without Lily asking first for 'O Little Town of Bethlehem.' It's now a Wright family tradition." Lily wrinkled her nose at him and poked him back.

Lily winked at Ken. "Another family tradition is you shaking all the gifts under the tree!"

Lydia Grace stared at Loretta before she started playing, and she could read Loretta's body language. She appeared to be enjoying the good-humored banter between Lily and Ken.

"Okay," said Lydia Grace, "let's begin with Lily's favorite, and as our guests, Cecilia, Gloria, and Loretta should choose next."

Lydia Grace and her dad began to play, and the others sang along. As one song ended, shouts for another favorite began.

Before long, it began to get dark. "Everyone, please keep singing," said Jerilyn. "I'm just going to heat up Thursday and Friday night's leftovers. We can all share a light supper together."

Lydia Grace, Carrie Emeline, Cecilia, Gloria, and Loretta rose and offered to help. Lily picked up Ellie from her swing, and said, "You have plenty of helpers, Mom, so I should take Ellie upstairs, nurse her, and put her to bed."

"You go right ahead, Lily," said Jerilyn. "I agree. There are plenty to help me."

Jerilyn and the five young ladies set the fried chicken, corn, green beans, mashed potatoes and gravy, cornbread and iced tea on the dining room table. The men returned the chairs, and everyone gathered around and held hands while Christopher asked the blessing.

"Dear Heavenly Father, we thank Thee for the wonderful bounty we are about to receive. I thank Thee that my family, friends, and new friends could be together for this occasion. It's a pleasure to meet Cecilia, Gloria, and Loretta, and have them spend this month, the special month of the celebration of Thy birth, with our family and friends. We thank Thee for the love and protection that surrounds our home and Christmas Hotel. In the precious name of Jesus we pray ... amen."

The others repeated their amens.

The expressions on the faces of Cecilia, Gloria, and Loretta touched Lydia Grace's heart. All three appeared ready to cry, and a tear did slide down Gloria's cheek. *There's a sadness surrounding these three. I wish I knew what was wrong, so I can try and help them. Help me to find a way, Jesus.*

Chapter Fifteen

Sunday Morning Service

"For all have sinned , and come short of the glory of God; Being justified freely by his grace through the redemption that is in Christ Jesus: Whom God hath set forth to be a propitiation through faith in his blood, to declare his righteousness for the remission of sins that are past, through the forbearance of God;"
Romans 3: 23-25

December 17, 1967
Back at Christmas Hotel, Gloria awakened, still tired, and aware she had not slept much the night before; even her head ached. As usual, her thoughts turned to Matthew, knowing she was in denial, and that he most likely was dead somewhere far away in Vietnam. Even the army had spent weeks trying to locate him before notifying the family that he was MIA. Her heart was having a hard time accepting this probable fact. She shuddered at the

overwhelming evidences, and wept again.

Wiping her eyes, she looked around her room. It was such an amazing hotel and there were so many people to get to know. After yesterday, she could tell that Ken enjoyed the company of Loretta, and Eugene likewise with Cecilia. She wondered how Cecilia and Loretta felt about the attention. Both girls were polite to the young men, but Gloria felt a sorrow surrounding Cecilia and Loretta. Sorrow was something all three of them had in common. She questioned why Cecilia and Loretta were here at Christmas Hotel. Were they trying to heal from some nightmare, too?

She knew Loretta attended the University of Cincinnati and shared a dorm room with Lydia Grace, so she wondered why Loretta didn't stay with Lydia Grace at the lovely Wright family home on South College Street. Like her, it was obvious Cecilia and Loretta were also in awe of the beautiful and historic residence. Christmas Hotel is lovely, but it was still a hotel. Why hadn't Loretta jumped at the opportunity to spend time with such a delightful family? Cecilia was different. Gloria knew nothing about her, except that she was from Houston, Texas. *I'm curious as to what secrets those two are hiding. But they're probably curious about me, too.*

*****

All three young ladies were dressed and ready for breakfast at six. They opened their doors at the same time and had to chuckle at the unplanned timing as they locked the doors behind them. They descended the beautiful cherry staircase of Christmas Hotel and walked toward the dining room.

"Oh, Miss Loretta," said Mr. Mullins, the manager on duty behind the front desk, "I was able to post your letter to Germany yesterday. The postmaster thinks it will arrive before Christmas."

"Thank you, sir," she said, continuing toward the dining room.

After they placed their breakfast orders, they all three acted nervous and uncomfortable. Finally, Gloria spoke. "Are you two going to accept the Wrights' invitation to attend the service this morning at the Methodist church on the square?"

Cecilia cleared her throat. "I don't want the church to receive a lightning bolt firing down from Heaven and burn to the ground, because I walk in. I haven't been to church since June fourth, the day I graduated high school."

Loretta snickered, and said, "I'd feel like such a hypocrite. I haven't been to church in an even longer time."

"Well, although I'm the daughter of a church deacon, I feel the same as you two," said Gloria.

"However, I was raised with the belief that no matter what sins you have in your past, you're still welcome in church. Even Christians will sin. They're just forgiven."

Cecilia and Loretta rolled their eyes at each other, but although Gloria saw their reactions, she continued anyway. "The Bible says Jesus welcomed all the sinners to come into His presence," Gloria added. "Okay, I realize it sounds corny to you and as though I'm preaching, but I'm not trying to do that. I just want you to know that I feel unworthy, too, but the Bible clearly says that all have sinned and come short of the glory of God. Our redemption comes from the blood of Jesus Christ."

She paused, and glanced from Cecilia to Loretta, trying to ascertain their feelings, but their faces gave little away. She would push it just a bit further "What else do we have to do on a Sunday in this little town?" she asked. "We may as well give church a try. We can sit in the back and leave if we feel like it."

The food arrived, and Loretta and Cecilia appeared deep in concentration while they ate. Finally, Cecilia opened up to the others. "I was raised in church, too. I suppose I can try it again."

Loretta turned toward Gloria and said, "My parents always took me to church while I was growing up." Then she paused. "Nothing is the same as it was three months ago," she added, with bitterness in her voice.

"I understand your anger," said Gloria nodding in agreement. "I miss Matthew, and I have anger, too. I'm bitter, distrusting, and in pain. I don't know if he's dead or alive." She addressed both of them. "I do know that going to church this morning can't hurt any of us. What do you say, Loretta? Can you give it a try?"

Loretta nodded reluctantly. "All right. Just don't be upset if I get up and walk out."

"I won't. That's why we'll sit on the back row with anyone else who wants to bolt. Visitors do that at home in my church all the time."

Breakfast over, they returned to their rooms to dress appropriately before leaving for the church.

*****

Together they walked across the square to 107 North College Street to the First Methodist Church of Franklin, where the Wrights said they would be. Beside one of the church's double doors, a church plaque with the date of 1911 was displayed, and outside the church stood a life-sized Nativity Scene. Smiling people nodded or said good morning to them before entering the church. The girls responded cordially with a smile or a nod to all that greeted them.

Lovely New Testament paintings adorned the

walls in the beautiful foyer, and the three were welcomed by the pastor and his wife. "Hello, ladies, I'm Pastor Joseph Palmer, and this is my wife Mary."

He laughed when he saw the expressions on their faces. "Yes, I, Joseph, married the lovely Mary. However, we named none of our five boys Jesus ... or our two girls Mary!" He laughed at his own joke. "We like to say we have a basketball team with two cheerleaders."

This time the three girls chuckled, too, along with any who overheard.

The pastor and his wife shook all their hands. "I don't recognize you, so you're probably staying at Christmas Hotel. Am I correct?" A big smile lit up his kind face.

"Yes," answered Gloria for all of them.

"Well, we're happy to have you join us. Please sit wherever you prefer."

"Thank you," said Gloria.

They walked into the church sanctuary, and the usher handed each of them a bulletin. Spotting enough room in the middle section in the last pew, the girls quickly sat before other back pew parishioners could lay claim to the pew. Cecilia sat next to the aisle, with Gloria in the middle, and Loretta on the other end. Gloria examined each of the exquisite stained glass windows, while Cecilia and Gloria read the bulletin.

Christopher, Jerilyn, and their family stretched across the front two rows in the middle section. Christopher turned in the pew and made eye contact after the three girls settled into their seats. He stood and walked back to them.

"Would you like to join us up in the front? There's plenty of room."

Loretta and Cecilia both glanced at Gloria, and she knew she would need to continue being the spokesperson for the three. Cecilia and Loretta quickly stared down in their laps and again pretended to read the pamphlet. "No, sir," Gloria answered. "We decided to sit back here, but thank you for asking."

"Well, I thank you three for coming. Maybe we can all have lunch at Christmas Hotel after the service."

At his invitation, Loretta and Cecilia looked up, gazed at Christopher and smiled. Gloria took their smiles as her cue and again answered for the three of them. "That would be lovely, Mr. Wright. We'd like that."

Christopher returned to his seat in the front pew with his family.

People walked by and smiled at the girls. Some of them even shook their hands and introduced themselves. Cecilia and Loretta squirmed in their seats, and although the attention clearly made them uncomfortable, they were polite. Gloria wasn't sure what denomination of church the other two attended, but she was used to this friendliness in her own home church in Gary, Indiana.

The adult choir sang a rousing "Hallelujah Chorus" from *The Messiah* while approximately thirty children quietly filed in, stood in front of the choir, and faced the congregation. When the choir finished their hymn, they sang with the children a selection of Christmas carols, beginning with "Hark! The Herald Angels Sing," then "Joy to the World", "God Rest Ye Merry, Gentlemen", "Do You Hear What I Hear?," and ending with "Silent Night."

Loretta and Cecilia faced forward, and their expressions appeared less stressed. *Dear Heavenly Father*, Gloria prayed, *You know everything about me. You know I love Matthew, and I'm scared. You and I are the only ones who know I'm pregnant. I don't know what to do. I know I have no right to ask for Your help, but I'm asking anyway. If You help me, please help Cecilia and Loretta in whatever troubles them. Please find a way for all of us. Amen.*

As the choir and the children filed out, Pastor Palmer asked the congregation to stand for the reading of God's word. "'For all have sinned, and come short of the glory of God; Being justified freely by his grace through the redemption that is in Christ Jesus: Whom God hath set forth to be a propitiation through faith in his blood, to declare his righteousness for the remission of sins that are past, through the forbearance of God.' Romans chapter three: verses twenty-three through twenty-five."

The three gawked at each other in amazement. That's basically what Gloria had said to Cecilia and Loretta earlier to encourage them to come to church. Gloria's thoughts ran rampant. *Are You trying to tell me something, Lord? This can't be a coincidence.* She sat quietly through the service, as did Cecilia and Loretta, none of them choosing to leave.

At the altar call, the congregation sang, "Turn Your Eyes Upon Jesus." Gloria sang along with the congregation the words she knew so well.

O soul, are you weary and troubled?
No light in the darkness you see?
There's light for a look at the Savior,
And life more abundant and free!

Pastor Palmer spoke to the congregation about salvation. "I implore all who are under conviction for their sins and want to know Jesus as their personal savior to come forward. I will take the Bible and show you what the Bible says regarding salvation. If any are already saved and feel led to rededicate your lives to Jesus, also come forward, and someone will pray with you.

Turn your eyes upon Jesus,
Look full in His wonderful face,
And the things of earth will grow strangely dim,
In the light of His glory and grace.

Gloria fought the urge to go forward and rededicate her life to Jesus. The tears began to roll down her cheeks. She knew that He was speaking to her. Her heart heard the conversation with Jesus.

I'm not ready, Jesus.

Yes, you are.

Matthew may be dead.

Does that mean you must stop loving and trusting Me?

I'm scared.

I'll be here for you.

I'm pregnant.

I know you are, and I know you aren't perfect.

What if I abort this baby? The baby should not be here. It's a mistake.

I knit that baby together in your womb. The

baby is precious in My sight. Babies are not mistakes. People are not perfect. They make mistakes. All babies have a purpose.

She cried harder. She reached into her purse and searched for a tissue. She couldn't find one. She could no longer see through the tears. Cecilia pressed a tissue into Gloria's hand.

"Thank you," Gloria said to her. "Excuse me." She stepped in front of Cecilia and ran down the aisle and knelt at the altar. Within seconds, she felt an arm go around her. She looked to her right, and through her tears, she saw Jerilyn. Gloria turned to Jerilyn and embraced her.

The congregation sang another hymn for those who remained at the altar.

"What's troubling you?" Jerilyn asked softly and with compassion.

Gloria softly blew her nose. In a hoarse whispered voice, she said, "I've said some terrible things about God, when Matthew was reported MIA." She paused. "That's not all. I'm pregnant with Matthew's child. I've considered abortion." She stopped and looked into Jerilyn's eyes for the shocked look, but saw no condemnation.

In a sympathetic voice, Jerilyn responded with, "I've been in a similar situation, but God always has another plan for all of his children. Can you trust Him to work this out for you?"

"I ... think so."

"Gloria, are you a Christian?"

"Yes. I asked the Lord to save me when I was nine. So did Matthew."

"Would you like to rededicate your life to the Lord, right here and now?"

This time, Gloria didn't hesitate. "Yes, I would."

"Then ask Him from your heart."

The words finally tumbled from her mouth, and the tears flowed freely down her cheeks. "Dear Heavenly Father, I have sinned. I have sinned against You, and I'm sorry. I have blamed You about Matthew. I have been so angry and bitter, and I'm sorry. Please forgive me. I rededicate my life to you today. I will wait for You to help me. I trust You, Lord Jesus. I will not abort my baby. I will trust that You have a plan for my baby and me. In the name of Jesus I pray ... amen".

Jerilyn echoed her amen.

Gloria hugged Jerilyn and together they rose from the altar; both smiling and wiping tears. Gloria looked to the back of the sanctuary and saw that much to her sorrow, Cecilia and Loretta were gone. She frowned in sadness, but Jerilyn placed her arm around her and led her to the Wright family pew. The congregation was singing the last paragraph and chorus of "At the Cross."

But drops of grief can ne'er repay
The debt of love I owe:
Here, Lord, I give myself away
'tis all that I can do.
At the cross, at the cross where I first saw the light,
And the burden of my heart rolled away,
It was there by faith I received my sight,
And now I am happy all the day!

Pastor Palmer asked one of the men to say a closing prayer. While the church prayed, he and his wife stood at the front door to say goodbye to the congregation as they filed out. The Wright family and Gloria thanked Pastor Palmer for the service and walked to Christmas Hotel.

Cecilia and Loretta did not show up for the noon meal.

Chapter Sixteen

Cecilia

"Cease from anger, and forsake wrath: fret not thyself in any wise to do evil.
For evildoers shall be cut off: but those that wait upon the Lord, they shall inherit the earth.
For yet a little while, and the wicked shall not be: yea, thou shalt diligently consider his place, and it shall not be."
Psalms 37: 8-10

Monday Morning, December 18, 1967
Cecilia tossed and turned in her bed all through the night. Not only did she skip the noon meal after the church service, but also the evening meal. She had no desire to speak to anyone. She was pleased for Gloria, that her life was on its way to getting back on track, but she knew that her own was still in turmoil. She also had to find a local doctor, because she was told to follow-up in two or three weeks with another appointment.

She needed to get out of the hotel and walk around. She didn't want to have breakfast in the Christmas Hotel dining room. She walked to the window and pulled open the heavy drapes. A light snow fell, but nothing to amount to anything. She had seen a little bakery on the way to church yesterday. She would get some donuts and hot chocolate.

After brushing her hair, teeth, and washing her face, she bundled up and quietly slipped out the front door of Christmas Hotel. She spoke to no one during the one-block walk, but hurried to Kwality Bakery on West Cedar Street. After purchasing two donuts and a cup of hot chocolate, she headed outside, where she chose a park bench on the west side of the square. She would have her back to Christmas Hotel. She just wanted to be alone.

As she ate the donuts and sipped the hot chocolate, her thoughts turned to yesterday's church service. She had been raised in a Southern Baptist church in Houston and could not remember a time when her parents didn't have her in church. "Every time the doors are open," her parents would say. Cecilia always considered herself the black sheep of the family. All her family, including her two younger brothers, were Christians. All except her. She realized she missed her parents and her brothers. When she finished the donuts, she let out a huge sigh.

I know I'm hurting my parents and my brothers, but I can't face them. I've done everything they don't believe in. They'd never forgive me. I just don't know what to do. I can't live off the generosity of the Woodsons' church forever. Maybe I should get a job here in Franklin. Yeah, right. What kind of reference do I have? I'm still in the Bible belt. I can say I graduated high school, but then I took off with my boyfriend, traveled to San Francisco, lived the life of a hippie in the Haight-Asbury neighborhood, drank a lot, smoked marijuana, and indulged in promiscuous sex. Oh yeah, not to forget I had an abortion. Wow … what a reference that would be! If Mr. and Mrs. Wright knew about me, they'd probably not allow me around their children and grandchildren.

Gloria asked forgiveness yesterday. I don't know what she did, but no one has been as bad as I have. God wouldn't forgive me. I know I wouldn't forgive me, so why should He? The redemption of a sin-filled life. That's what they preach about. Ha! Maybe that's for people who lied, stole, or cheated on a test. Here, I'm only eighteen, and I've done about everything wrong. I certainly didn't turn out the way my parents raised me. They'd be better off without me in their lives. If I was dead, my problems would be over, and my parents would be free of their problem child.

"Is this seat taken?"

Cecilia jumped, spilling the last swallow of hot

chocolate on the hem of her coat.

"I'm sorry. I didn't mean to frighten you." Eugene removed a handkerchief from his pocket and dabbed at the spill, wiping away all traces of the chocolate. "It's gone," he said with a big smile. "If I'm forgiven, may I join you?"

"It's okay, Eugene. It's good that my coat is brown. It'll never show. You can sit with me."

"You were so deep in thought and looked so serious. What's a young lady like you have to be so thoughtful about?"

"At the moment, I don't feel like an eighteen-year old young lady. I feel like I'm at least twenty-five."

"Ouch! That hurt. I'm twenty-seven."

"Sorry."

"Sorry that you cut me to the core, or that I'm such an old man?" He held his chest feigning a heart attack.

Cecilia laughed. "You *are* amusing, Eugene."

"Oh, you find me amusing, do you? So I'm old, and now I'm amusing."

"You're a nice guy, Eugene. Why aren't you married?"

"Wow ... you get right to the point. I guess I've never found the right woman to put up with me."

"Do you have bad habits?"

"Let me see. I don't smoke, carouse or use foul

language. Bad habits, huh? I'm not really neat. I can be messy. I spill things." He looked at her coat and they both laughed. "I teach algebra and gcomctry at Franklin-Simpson High School here in town. My students tell me I win the award for the messiest teacher's desk. I always reply that I know where everything is. That's not always true, so I guess you could say I sometimes fib. However, I'm loyal and trustworthy. I should have been a Boy Scout."

"Why weren't you?"

"Well, that's a long story."

"I've got plenty of time. I don't have anywhere to go, unless you do."

"No. School's out, so I have plenty of time until January second when classes resume." He cocked his head. "Would you really like to hear, or are you just making polite conversation?"

Cecilia smiled and said with deliberate sincerity, "I'd really like to hear."

"Okay, you asked for it." He paused, as though considering where to begin. "I'll give you the abbreviated version. You met my parents on Saturday, and my siblings. My siblings are by blood, but my parents aren't. All four of us were adopted by Darius and Barbara Scott around this time, thirteen years ago. You could say that all of us received a Christmas miracle. My adoptive parents were childless and wanted children, and our biological parents had four children and didn't want us."

Cecilia knew the look on her face must have been surprise. She was fortunate to have loving parents who wanted all three of their children. "I ... don't understand ... you know, not wanting you."

"Most people don't understand. In fact, before we met the Wrights, and later the Scotts, my sisters, brother, and I didn't understand any other way of life. We were used to being slapped around, cursed at, told we were worthless no-nothing brats, or just ignored. We lived with our biological parents in Bowling Green at the time, growing up in a seedy apartment above a billiard parlor."

"Where's Bowling Green?"

"Sorry, I forgot you were from Houston. Bowling Green is twenty-two miles north of Franklin. Let me see," he said while stroking his chin, "where do I go from here? Our biological parents are Otto and Eula Mae Smith, and three years ago they each completed a ten-year sentence for child abuse. They nearly killed me in one beating, along with one other child. The last I heard, they were living somewhere in Eastern Kentucky. I know that Otto was originally from Clay County, so he has kin-folk there. Why they had four children, I'll never know. They were on the government dole, so I suppose we were a commodity. I don't ever remember either of them doing a lick of work. They lived off the government system and the good people at churches."

"Have you seen Otto and Eula Mae since they were released?"

"No, I haven't. I was called Junior at the time, but after our adoption by the Scotts, I no longer wanted to be associated with Otto. His name was Otto Eugene, and I was Otto Eugene Smith, Junior. Therefore, when the Scotts adopted us, I decided I would go by Eugene Scott. I became a Christian shortly after the adoption, and so did my other three siblings. I'm an active member of the Methodist church in Bowling Green with Darius and Barbara Scott, and I consider them my parents. I have no desire to see Otto and Eula Mae. They're a bad part of my past. You asked why I never became a Boy Scout. Otto and Eula Mae never provided me with the opportunity. "

"I'm glad you told me," Cecilia said softly and pondered his words. *Maybe I have something in common with Otto and Eula Mae. After all, I didn't want my baby either. Am I just as bad as them? I did take the life of my baby. I can't help but wonder: is there is a difference if the baby is in the womb or out? Does it matter? Is a baby in the womb even important?*

Chapter Seventeen

Dr. Beasley

"Thanks be unto God for his unspeakable gift."
2 Corinthians 9:15

Tuesday Morning December 19, 1967
Loretta awakened to a dreary, snowy, and cloudy morning; Exactly the mood she was in. For a brief moment the frat party and Barry seemed like a fading nightmare, then reality struck home. A living nightmare. *Pregnant!*

Not only will I have to put up with perky Lydia Grace while I'm here, but now Gloria, too. I hope Gloria doesn't think she's all high and mighty after Sunday morning. I'm not sure I even know what happened with her. Did she join up with these Bible-toting people down here? Cecilia must have known what was happening, when she handed Gloria the tissue. I don't even care to know. I just want to get this – whatever it is – out of me. I'll talk to Mr. Wright about a doctor in this one-horse town. I wonder if they even have a doctor here. I hope I won't have to hitch a ride to Nashville.

She dressed and descended the staircase. She strode straight to the front desk and addressed Christopher, who was working. "Does this town have a doctor?"

"Yes, we have a fine doctor, and his name is Dr. Beasley." His pause was brief. "Please don't think I'm invading your privacy, but are you ill?"

He showed such concern that Loretta forgot about her earlier sour mood. She responded in a cordial voice. "No, sir. I ... a ... just need some advice," she stammered. "Do you have his phone number?"

"Yes, Loretta, I do." He walked to his Rolodex on the counter behind him, and rotated the index cards until he found Dr. Beasley. He wrote down the number on a piece of Christmas Hotel stationery.

"Thank you." She looked at the number, puzzled. "There are only five digits."

"That's correct. Here in Franklin, you'll only need to dial a six, which is the final number in our five-eight-six exchange, and the final four digits of your party's phone number. You probably had to dial all seven digits in Cincinnati. It's a large city with many more exchanges."

"Yes, you're right. Again, thank you. I'm just going to go to my room and call his office." She ran up the staircase, entered her room, and bolted the door. She hurried to the phone by her bed and dialed the number.

"Dr. Beasley's Clinic," said the receptionist, in a pleasant soft southern accent.

"My name is Loretta Jenkins, and I'd like to make an appointment with the doctor."

"We had several cancellations this morning from our older patients due to the snow and the fog. Could you manage to get here at nine-thirty?"

"Yes, nine-thirty would be fine."

"What may I record for the reason of this appointment?"

"A ... pregnancy."

"Okay, Mrs. Jenkins, we will see you at nine-thirty."

"The name is *Miss* Jenkins."

There was a slight hesitancy on the other end, but the receptionist recovered quickly. "I'll make the correction and see you at nine-thirty, Miss Jenkins. The address is one-fifteen South College Street."

Loretta showered, dressed, and was out the door at nine o'clock.

*****

Gloria slept badly, her mind filled with thoughts of Matthew, lost, dead, or prisoner of the enemy in Vietnam. The nightmares all night long gave her a headache. She sat up slowly, rubbing her temples. There was no point lying in bed and wondering. She needed to be doing something. Suddenly and unexpectedly the peace of Jesus swept over her. She recalled how she had gone to the altar and rededicated her life to Jesus. It was real. It was wonderful. It was forever. She broke into a smile and clapped her hands. "*Yes!*"

Now in a much better mood, she decided this might be a good day to see a doctor and follow-up on the care of herself and the baby. She dressed and hurried down the stairs at Christmas Hotel and walked to the front desk.

"Good morning, Mr. Wright," she said in a pleasant voice, with a smile on her face. "I was wondering if you had the name and phone number of a good doctor in Franklin."

He regarded her with some puzzlement on his face. She wasn't sure why he held that expression, but she didn't want to go into details regarding the pregnancy. Obviously, Mrs. Wright had not betrayed her confidence. She accepted the name and number on the piece of paper, and noted he did not even need to look up the number.

As she accepted the piece of paper, he told her that she only needed to dial the last five digits in Franklin. Most likely, in Gary, Indiana, she had to dial seven digits, as it was a bigger city with more exchanges.

She nodded, thanked him, and hurried upstairs to dial the phone number.

She entered her room and closed the door. Her phone was on the nightstand by her bed, but she stretched the phone and the long coiled cord over to the desk so that she could write. She dialed the five digits on the rotary desk phone.

"Dr. Beasley's Clinic," the receptionist announced.

"Good morning. I'd like to make an appointment to see the doctor."

"He's had some cancellations this morning, but if you can come in at ten o'clock, he can see you then."

"That would be fine."

"May I get your name and record the reason for the appointment?"

"My name is Gloria Reynolds, and an out of state doctor determined that I'm a little more than two months pregnant. The doctor said I would need a follow-up appointment at this time."

"Yes, you do, Mrs. Reynolds. We'll see you at ten o'clock."

"Actually ... it's *Miss* Reynolds."

The hesitation was only for a couple of seconds, but Gloria noticed. "All right, Miss Reynolds. I'll adjust the record and see you at ten o'clock." She gave Gloria the address.

Gloria showered, dressed, and was out the door by nine-thirty.

*****

Cecilia awakened and walked to the window, drawing the drapes. *Well, what a foggy, snowy, and dreary day. I guess today is as good as any to have that follow-up doctor's appointment. I don't have anything else to do. My dance card is not exactly filled.* "Ha, ha!" she said aloud.

She showered, threw on some jeans and a sweater, descended the staircase, and marched up to the front desk. The pain in her womb had eased over the past couple of days.

"Good morning, Cecilia," Mr. Wright said, with a pleasant smile.

"Good morning, Mr. Wright," she replied in a terse voice. "Would you happen to have the name and phone number of a doctor here in Franklin?"

He frowned and shot her the strangest look.

"Cecilia, has the food here at Christmas Hotel been acceptable? Have there been any problems?"

"No, sir, everything is fine. I just need to see the doctor on a personal matter."

"Oh, I was a bit alarmed, because you're the third guest this morning to ask for the name and phone number of our town's doctor." Not having to look up the number, he wrote the information on the Christmas Hotel stationery and handed it to her with the five digit speech.

"Thanks, Mr. Wright," she said, and turned and hurried up the staircase.

She entered her room, threw her key on the desk, and dialed the five digits.

"Dr. Beasley's Clinic," said the pleasing voice that answered.

"Hello, my name is Miss Cecilia Edmondson, and I would like to have an appointment with the doctor. Does he have something available today or tomorrow?"

"He had several cancellations this morning, I just filled two, but I still have one appointment left at ten-thirty. Would you like that appointment?"

"Yes, that'll work."

"May I ask the reason ... for the appointment?" Cecilia heard hesitancy in the voice for some unknown reason.

"I need to have a follow-up appointment ... on a surgical procedure ... I had recently." Cecilia was not sure what to call this appointment, and the words just came out haltingly.

Cecilia thought she heard relief in the woman's voice. "I will see you at ten-thirty," the woman said. She gave Cecilia the address.

Cecilia was out the door by ten o'clock.

*****

Loretta arrived in plenty of time. She passed the Wrights' home as she briskly walked along South College Street, but didn't see anyone she knew. She walked into the clinic, stamped the snow from her boots on the doormat, and headed to the receptionist's window. She read the name on the window plaque: Bettye Sue Tuck.

"Hi ... er ... Bettye Sue," she recited from the plaque. "I'm Loretta Jenkins, and I have an appointment at nine-thirty."

Bettye Sue smiled. "Yes, I spoke with you on the phone earlier. I just need you to fill out these papers, and then Dr. Beasley will see you."

Loretta chose a seat and filled in the papers with her parents' address. *After all, it's still my home.*

She returned the papers back to Bettye Sue who asked her to take a seat, and she would be called back shortly.

She hadn't been seated long, when Bettye Sue said, "Miss Jenkins, would you please come back to the window?"

When Loretta appeared, Bettye Sue said, "I just noticed that you recorded your address in Cincinnati, Ohio."

"Yes, ma'am. That's my family home, but I'm spending time at Christmas Hotel while I'm on Christmas vacation from the University of

Cincinnati. I was told to have a follow-up at this time, so I need to see a doctor while I'm here. Is there a problem?"

"No, not at all. I just wanted to clarify the out-of-state address."

Loretta returned to her seat, selected a magazine left over from the summer, and absent mindedly thumbed through it. Two women sat across from her on the other side of the waiting room. She was unable to see them, because a large planter divided the room. Although the women spoke softly, Loretta couldn't help hearing the conversation.

"Jerilyn, I want to thank you for coming with me today. I'm so nervous, and with James out of town this week on business, I just didn't want to be alone. He offered to cancel his business trip, but I told him I'd be fine. We need the money. I don't make a lot waitressing at the diner in the bus station, although the tips are good."

"It's okay, Carol Ann. I was happy to come with you."

Carol Ann ... a waitress at the diner in the bus station, and she's here with Jerilyn Wright.

"It's just that I didn't want to be alone when I got the tests back. James and I want children so badly. I've now had three miscarriages. I don't know what I'll do if I can't have children."

"Hopefully, Carol Ann, it's just stress. I had miscarriages twice. Both little boys. I know each miscarriage was due to stress, because I was still depressed from when Lydia Grace was kidnapped after her birth."

"Unfortunately, Jerilyn, I think my miscarriages are due to another reason. A reason I deeply regret."

Lydia Grace was kidnapped at birth? I wonder how long she was missing before she was found. Maybe I've misjudged Lydia Grace. It's just that she's so happy all the time.

A door opened. "Good morning, Carol Ann. Dr. Beasley is ready for you. James couldn't come?"

"Good morning, Jane. No, he offered to cancel a business trip, but I said I'd be okay. Do you mind if Jerilyn comes back with me?"

"Not at all, Carol Ann. Dr. Beasley will see you in his office to go over the tests."

A few minutes later the nurse returned. "Miss Jenkins?"

Her name tag said Jane Wilson, RN, and Loretta followed her to an examining room. "I see you're here regarding your pregnancy. Have you seen a doctor?"

"Yes, I saw a doctor in Cincinnati. He confirmed I was pregnant and gave me a due date of July fourth. How about that ... Independence Day,"

Loretta said rather sarcastically.

"It doesn't appear that you are pleased about your baby."

"Good assumption! If I knew where to get an abortion, that's where I'd be right now."

Jane winced, and Loretta realized how callous she must sound. Nurse Wilson took Loretta's blood pressure, then opened a cabinet and handed Loretta a clean gown and a sheet for her body.

"Please undress and put on this gown. Then you can lie down on the examination table, put your feet in the stirrups, and cover up with this sheet. I will return with Dr. Beasley shortly."

Before the doctor and nurse entered, Loretta heard a woman walking down the hall, crying, and heard Jerilyn Wright say, "Carol Ann, do you want me to call James and ask him to come home?"

"No, he needs to be on this business trip. It's entirely my fault that I'll never carry a baby."

"Well, I'm going to stay with you tonight, and I won't take no for an answer. You need a friend right now."

"Thank you, Jerilyn."

She heard a door open and close. *They must have returned to the waiting room. I'm sorry she can't conceive. I wish she was carrying this baby and not me.*

A moment later her door opened, and Nurse

Wilson entered with a man around sixtyish. He smiled at her. "I'm Dr. Beasley. I see from the information you gave my nurse that you're just past two months pregnant, confirmed by a doctor in Cincinnati. Are you planning on returning to Cincinnati?"

"Yes, when this Christmas vacation is over. I'm here because Lydia Grace Wright invited me. I suppose you know her. I've only been here a few days, but everyone seems to know the locals."

"That's correct. This is a friendly town with very good people in it. People here help each other."

Loretta thought about Jerilyn helping Carol Ann, and also Gloria on Sunday morning at church. "Well, I won't be here long enough to concern myself with this town and its people," she said in a brusque manner.

"You appear bitter, Miss Jenkins. Is there something wrong with people helping people?" he asked, while he washed his hands.

"If that's what you want to call it, Doc. Why don't you just get on with the examination of me, *and* this *thing* in my body?"

He stared at her – a bit annoyed, Loretta thought.

He held up his hands, Nurse Wilson dried them, and put Dr. Beasley's latex gloves on him.

The examination did not take long. Dr. Beasley

removed the gloves, and tossed them in the trash dispenser.

"Miss Jenkins, your *baby* is developing just fine," said Dr. Beasley. "You appear to be fine, too. Did your doctor in Cincinnati give you prenatal vitamins, and do blood work on you?"

"Yes, he did." Loretta could tell he was perturbed with her, but she had to admit that he maintained his professionalism. Loretta actually liked him. He certainly didn't allow her to walk all over him, and he refused to take her lip. "I've been taking the vitamins and extra iron. I was low on iron."

He reached up in the cabinet, shuffled some pictures and pulled one out. "You are around nine to ten weeks pregnant. Here's a picture of the baby now. You can take this with you. You'll see that your baby has a body and all its fingers and toes. It is *not* a thing. Think about that, Miss Jenkins."

At that he turned and started to walk out. He stopped, spun around, and said, "You may get dressed, Miss Jenkins. You'll need another appointment in six weeks, wherever you are at that time. Before you leave, please see Mrs. Tuck our receptionist. Good day." He and Nurse Wilson exited the room.

Loretta stuck the picture in her purse without looking at it. She dressed and headed to the receptionist's desk, where she paid Bettye Sue, and said she wouldn't need another appointment. As she started toward the door, she saw Gloria filling out paperwork.

"Hello, Gloria. Fancy meeting you here."

Gloria looked up, and her expression turned to surprise. "Yes. Small world, huh?"

"See you back at Christmas Hotel." She opened the door and left before Gloria could say anything else.

*****

Gloria rose and handed the paperwork to Mrs. Tuck. Bettye Sue glanced at it. "I see you're from Gary, Indiana. Are you by any chance staying at Christmas Hotel?"

"Yes, ma'am, I am," Gloria answered politely.

"Are you on Christmas vacation from a university?"

"No, ma'am. I'm here for my own rest. I'm not sure yet how long I'll be residing in Franklin. My fiancé is stationed in Vietnam." She wasn't going to say he was MIA. Maybe she should tell the doctor though. Yes, of course she would, when the time was right.

"Please have a seat, and Nurse Wilson will call you shortly."

Within a few minutes, Nurse Wilson appeared at the door, "Miss Reynolds, would you come on back please? I'm Nurse Wilson."

"Pleased to meet you," Gloria responded with a smile.

"I see you're here to follow-up from another doctor regarding your pregnancy. Did he give you a due date?"

"Yes, it's July seventh. He gave me prenatal vitamins, and he did blood work. He asked me to get another appointment around this time to make certain everything was progressing normally. Mr. Wright at Christmas Hotel recommended Dr. Beasley."

"I'm going to check your blood pressure, and then you can undress and put on this gown and use this sheet for a cover." She handed the items to Gloria.

Nurse Wilson was quiet while she took Gloria's blood pressure. "Your blood pressure is very good at one-ten over seventy-seven. After you finish undressing, please lie down and put your feet in the stirrups. I'll return with Dr. Beasley shortly."

Nurse Wilson left the room, and Gloria followed the instructions.

Within five minutes, Nurse Wilson returned and introduced the doctor. "Miss Reynolds, this is Dr. Beasley," she said with a smile.

"It's nice to meet you, Dr. Beasley," Gloria said, while offering her hand from where she lay.

He shook it. "It's very nice to meet you, too, Miss Reynolds."

He walked to the sink, washed his hands, and Nurse Wilson dried them and pulled on the gloves.

After about five minutes, he said, "Please get dressed, and I'll be back directly."

When he returned, he asked, "How have you been feeling, Miss Reynolds?"

"Fine. Is something wrong with the baby?" Gloria asked, alarmed.

"No, the baby seems fine. I just wanted to know how *you* are."

"I appreciate your concern, Dr. Beasley. I know you're probably concerned because I'm not married. I must admit that I'm having some mental anguish. My fiancé Matthew is in the United States Army, and he was sent to Vietnam. His helicopter crashed on October thirtieth, and now he's MIA. My pregnancy was confirmed on December first. I had thoughts of abortion."

She saw the pain cross Dr. Beasley and Nurse Wilson's faces. "Don't worry, I've gotten past those thoughts. Matthew's father is a pastor and my father is a deacon in his church. I was bitter for a while. I came here to Christmas Hotel, because that's where both my parents and Matthew's parents had a joint honeymoon. I came here to heal. I've been depressed. Two days ago at Pastor

Palmer's church I rededicated my life to Jesus. No matter what happens, I'll be fine. In my heart I know that Matthew may very well be dead. I've heard the details as to what happened to him. I definitely *won't* take the life of Matthew's baby. I've loved him all my life." She began to cry, and Nurse Wilson handed her a box of tissues.

"Thank you."

"You're a brave young lady," said Dr. Beasley, as he patted her hand. "I believe you and your baby will be just fine. Would you like to see what your baby looks like in this stage of development?"

"Yes, I would. Thank you!"

He opened the cabinet and found the correct picture. "You are at approximately nine or ten weeks. This is what your baby looks like in the womb."

She studied the picture, and finally said, "He has very distinct features. He's a miniature newborn. Why, I thought he would still be a blob of plasma ... or a fish-like creature!" she added in amazement. "He even has eyelids and earlobes. He ... or she ... is amazing!"

"Yes, Miss Reynolds, I agree. The baby rapidly growing in your body *is* amazing. Why even at only twenty days past conception, the baby has a primitive heartbeat, but it's indeed a human heartbeat. Currently, your baby is just past an inch long with all the features in the picture. He or she is just very tiny."

"Dr. Beasley, thank you so much. I will treasure this picture," she said while holding it to her heart.

"You're quite welcome, Miss Reynolds."

They left the room and Gloria dressed. She literally bounced up to the receptionist's desk. "Hi, Mrs. Tuck, I'm ready to pay you," she said, still smiling.

"Would you like another appointment, Miss Reynolds?"

"I don't know how long I'll be in town, but I'll let you know if I stay. I might return to Gary, Indiana.

"Have a wonderful day, Miss Reynolds."

"You have a wonderful day, too, Mrs. Tuck."

When Gloria turned to leave, she saw Cecilia filling out paperwork. "Good morning, Cecilia," she said with a broad smile.

Cecilia looked up. "Good morning to you, too, Gloria."

"I'll see you back at Christmas Hotel. Have a wonderful day, Cecilia."

Gloria was out the door before Cecilia could respond.

*****

Cecilia returned the paperwork to Bettye Sue Tuck who glanced at the information. "I see your address is Houston, Texas. Are you staying at Christmas Hotel?"

"Yes, I am. Is it a problem I'm from out of town?"

"No, it's not a problem at all, Miss Edmondson. Please have a seat, and Nurse Wilson will call you shortly.

Within a minute, Cecilia heard, "Miss Edmondson, you may come back now."

Cecilia examined the woman's name tag. Jane Wilson, RN. *Well, I suppose I'm in good hands.*

Cecilia followed Nurse Wilson into the examination room. "It says here that you're here for a follow-up on a surgery. When was the surgery?"

"December first."

"Where was the surgery performed?"

"In Houston, Texas."

"What hospital?"

"It wasn't in a hospital."

Nurse Wilson stared at her and frowned, obviously bewildered. Finally she asked, "Why did you have a surgery?"

"It wasn't *exactly* a surgery. I had an abortion."

"Oh."

There was no denying Nurse Wilson's different facial expressions, of surprise, unbelief, and then no expression at all, as she processed the information. Finally Nurse Wilson asked, "How far along were you when you had the abortion?"

"Around three months, give or take a couple of weeks."

Nurse Wilson appeared to be trying her best to maintain an expression of indifference, but she wasn't succeeding.

"It's not really a baby at three months. I don't see the problem," said Cecilia nonchalantly.

Nurse Wilson didn't respond to her statement. She went about her duties in a very professional manner. She took Cecilia's blood pressure, handed her a clean gown and cover-up, and asked her to place her feet in the stirrups. "I'll return shortly with Dr. Beasley."

Cecilia was ready when Dr. Beasley entered with Nurse Wilson. Nurse Wilson stood back as Dr. Beasley introduced himself. "Good morning, I'm Dr. Beasley. Nurse Wilson tells me you had an abortion on December first, and you were approximately three months pregnant, give or take a couple of weeks. Is that correct?"

"Yes, that's correct."

"Have you seen a *real* doctor since?"

"Yes, just before I left Houston. He prescribed antibiotics, which I did take."

Dr. Beasley washed his hands, and Nurse Wilson dried and placed his gloves on. The examination was brief.

"Please get dressed, Miss Edmondson, and I'll return shortly."

They left the room.

I certainly hope I'm not going to get another lecture. It's not even a baby at eight to fourteen weeks, or however long I was pregnant.

When he returned, he didn't have a smile on his face. "You appear to be fine and good health. I don't know who performed your abortion, but it was probably illegal, if in Houston. Am I correct, Miss Edmondson?"

"Yes, it was in Houston."

"I'm nearly sixty years old, and I know where this country is headed. I realize that currently four states have legalized abortion under certain conditions. I predict the whole country will soon follow in that direction. I took an oath to save lives, and that includes the unborn."

He paused, then added, "I'm not here to chastise you, but I have a deep concern for you, too. Even if you were in a clean hospital, you could have died from infection, or your uterine wall could have ripped during the procedure. I have a patient who was your age when she had an abortion. Her uterine wall is weakened, and she will *never* carry a child to term. She is now married and desperately wants a child. She can't have one. She has had several miscarriages. I pray that doesn't happen to you, Miss Edmondson."

He pursed his lips, and shook his head slowly. "If you should find yourself in this situation again, there is another alternative. You can carry the child to term and give the baby up for adoption. It could save your life, *and* increase your chances of carrying a future child to term. *And* of course it would definitely save the life of the child. I could show you a picture of what your baby looked like at around three months, but I won't. It would only break your heart. Good day, Miss Edmondson."

At that, the doctor and the nurse left the room, closing the door firmly behind them.

Cecilia sat stunned for a moment. *Why don't they want me to see the picture of the fetus? After all, it's not a baby in the first trimester. Now, I've had two doctors tell me how my body may be damaged. Is it possible I might never have a child? Nah! They're probably exaggerating and trying to scare me.*

She dressed, paid the receptionist, and walked out.

Chapter Eighteen

Gloria

"And again, I will put my trust in him.
And again, Behold I and the children
which God hath given me."
Hebrews 2:13

Wednesday Morning, December 20, 1967
Gloria awakened and her first thoughts were of Matthew, and then the Lord Jesus and then her parents. *There will probably never come a day that I won't think of Matthew when I awaken, Jesus. At least now I think of You, too. I thank You, Jesus, for always being there for me. I had better write Mom and Dad a letter. They need to know everything that's happened. I know that they are probably worried sick about me. They need to know everything ... including my pregnancy. It's time. No more secrets. If I post a letter to them today, they may receive it on Saturday and before Christmas.*

She sat down at the desk, retrieved the Christmas Hotel stationery, a pen, and began to write.

December 20, 1967

Dear Mom and Dad,
I know you both have probably been worried about me since I left on December twelfth. Thank you for allowing me the space, which I needed. The first thing I want to say is how sorry I am for the way I treated you before I left. For that I am ashamed, and I hope you will forgive me.

I have met some of the most wonderful people. You already know Christopher and Jerilyn Wright. They are an amazing couple. They have five delightful children. Lily is the oldest and she's married to John Demeter. They both are teachers in nearby Russellville, Kentucky, and have four children. The Wrights also have twenty-five-year-old twins, Ken and Carrie Emeline. Ken teaches at the University of Kentucky, and Carrie Emeline teaches at the grade school in nearby Bowling Green, Kentucky.

The Wrights' youngest daughter, Lydia Grace is twenty-one and a student at the University of Cincinnati. She's there for the

Conservatory of Music, and she's an amazing pianist and composer! Their youngest child is twelve-year-old Chris, who says he will one day take over the management of Christmas Hotel. He's here just about every day, working in one capacity or another. He's very dedicated in learning all about Christmas Hotel, whether it's cleaning rooms, cooking, working the front desk or the dining room.

I have met two other girls who are also here alone and staying at Christmas Hotel. Loretta Jenkins attends the University of Cincinnati with Lydia Grace, and she arrived at the invitation of Lydia Grace for Christmas vacation. Loretta's parents died in a car accident on October first. She has an older brother who is in the United States Air Force, and he's stationed in Germany. She's in room #10 and I'm in room #9. The other girl is Cecilia Edmondson who is in room #8. Cecilia is from Houston, Texas. Her parents are living, and she has two little brothers. That's all I know about either of them. I do know there is a sadness surrounding each girl, but I don't know what it is. I've met other lovely people, too numerous to name.

I know you'll be pleased when you hear this next statement. Last Sunday I went to church, and I rededicated my life to Jesus. I have been so miserable since I heard about Matthew. However, I finally realize that no matter what happens to Matthew or me, He holds my hand. I can lean on Him. I will put the trust for my future in the Lord Jesus, and not in Matthew.

I don't know how you're going to feel about this next piece of information. The night before Matthew left, we married ourselves before God. Yes, I know it's not legal without a marriage license and a preacher, but in our hearts we were married. I feel married now, although I can't use Matthew's name. I know it's wrong in the eyes of the world, and the church. I'm not going to condone what we did, but I'm not going to spend my life apologizing either. I love Matthew, and I'm going to have his baby. That's the other reason I needed to get away. I didn't want people constantly asking me if I had an update on Matthew. I didn't want them to see my growing pregnancy and shy away from me or shun me or treat you two differently.

When I left home, I considered an abortion. Don't worry, those thoughts are now long gone. I will bring this child into the world. If God wants me to raise my child, I will. If not, he or she will be placed for adoption. Outside of Mrs. Wright, a doctor I saw in Gary, Indiana, and Dr. Beasley whom I saw here in Franklin, you are the first to know about the baby. Please pray with me, as to what will be best for my baby and your grandchild.

I don't know when I'll be home. I'm feeling a tug on my heart to stay here a while longer. I don't know how long that will be. I would like to be of help to Loretta and Cecilia in some capacity.

Please share this letter with Matthew's parents. I hope they are able to lean on God through this terrible ordeal regarding Matthew. And of course phone me here immediately at Christmas Hotel if you hear anything at all from the army, whether it's good news or bad news.

Merry Christmas, and I love you both very much. Gloria

She smiled as she folded the letter. *I feel better now that they will know everything. I don't like keeping secrets from my parents.* She decided not to put it in the Christmas Hotel envelope. She would go and buy a Christmas card for her parents and put the letter in with the card.

As soon as she was dressed, she hurried down the staircase and headed for the front desk. Chris was on duty this morning. "Good morning, Chris. I see your parents have you working the front desk today."

"Yes, Miss Gloria. In fact, the front desk is my favorite position. I like to talk to the guests as they come and go."

"I'm sure you're a wonderful asset for your parents. I need to know where I can get a Christmas card."

"Well, the Shugart and Willis Drugstore is right next door to us. They don't *just* carry drug store items. They would have some Christmas cards. Bring the card back here, and I'll put it out for the afternoon post."

"Thank you, Chris. I'll do that. See you shortly," and out the door she hurried.

As Gloria opened the door to the drug store, Cecilia walked out. The door bumped Cecilia's hand, and her sack fell on the ground. The contents of the sack rolled out on the sidewalk. Gloria stooped to pick up the pack of chewing gum and a large bottle of one hundred sleeping pills. She handed the items back to Cecilia.

"I'm just having a little trouble sleeping," Cecilia mumbled nervously. "I thought I'd pick up something to help."

Cecilia rushed back to Christmas Hotel.

"Hmm, that was strange," Gloria said aloud to herself.

She located the Christmas card rack, chose and paid for the card, and returned to Christmas Hotel. She noticed Loretta standing at the end of the counter talking to Chris and Ken, and didn't want to interrupt. She headed into the lobby and sat on one of the chairs by the Christmas tree, where she addressed the card and added the letter to her parents. After placing the card in the outgoing mail basket, she waved at the three of them and hurried up to her room.

Chapter Nineteen

Loretta

"A merry heart doeth good like a medicine:
but a broken spirit drieth the bones."
Proverbs 17:22

Wednesday late morning, December 20, 1967
"You have to have lunch, so you may as well have it with me," schmoozed Ken to Loretta, as he winked at his little brother.

"My brother's right," said Chris, taking the hint. "We don't want any of our *special* guests passing out from hunger."

Loretta had to laugh in spite of herself. "Okay, you both win. Are we eating here at Christmas Hotel?"

"Actually, I thought I'd take you somewhere different. There's a little place over on Kentucky Street that I like called ... drums please ..." Chris pretended to pound air drums for Ken, "Kentucky Grill."

"You're both nuts. Okay, I'll give it a try."

"Goodbye, little brother," Ken smiled, and

mouthed "thank you" to Chris.

Chris winked at him, and Loretta laughed again. "You two are in cahoots."

"Well, we *are* brothers," said Ken, as he took her arm and guided her to the front door.

Once outside, Ken walked on the street-side of the sidewalk with Loretta's arm linked in his.

"Are you always such a gentleman?" she asked, as she tilted her head and looked up at him. She was barely five feet tall, and he looked at least six feet tall, and maybe even an inch or two past.

"My parents raised me. If I had ever stepped out of line with a lady, I would not have been able to sit down for a week!"

"Were your parents overly strict?"

"No. They wanted me to grow up to be a man of whom they could be proud. I don't regret being raised by them. When I left home I attended the University of Kentucky, where, as you know, I now teach. When I was a student, most of the other students in my freshman class joined fraternities. I thought it was just an excuse to party and drink. I was there to learn. I stayed away from that crowd."

Loretta took a long look at Ken. *Are there really men like Ken in the world? If he's for real, why couldn't I have met him before I met Barry? That's stupid. If I hadn't met Barry, I wouldn't be rooming with Lydia Grace, and she wouldn't have invited me to Christmas Hotel. I would never have met Ken. The path of life is strange. It seems like one incident can change the course of an entire life. How strange is that? Now I'm thinking like that movie "It's a Wonderful Life."*

They arrived at the Kentucky Grill, and Ken held the door for her. "You got quiet," said Ken, as he led her to a table by the window, pulled out her chair, and seated her.

"I don't want to give you the big head, but I was wondering if considerate guys like you are for real."

He smiled at her, but didn't have a chance to answer. The waitress brought the menus. "What can I get you to drink?" she asked.

"I'll have a coke," said Loretta.

"Make that two," said Ken.

"What do you recommend, since this *is* your favorite place?"

"I didn't say it was my *favorite* place, but I do come here whenever I'm in town. It's unfortunate, because I hear they're closing at the end of the year. I guess others don't like it as much as I do. However, in answer to your question, I like the grilled pork tenderloin sandwich with french fries and slaw."

"Oh, that sounds yummy! Fattening, but scrumptious."

"I'll tell the cook to remove the calories before

the food is delivered," Ken said, and winked at her.

She laughed. "I was right, you *are* nuts."

The waitress returned, and Ken ordered for both of them.

Loretta stared into Ken's twinkling blue eyes. "You know, I haven't laughed much since I left UC and been in Franklin, but you've given me a reason to laugh several times today."

"It's important to laugh. To quote Proverbs chapter seventeen, verse twenty-two: 'A merry heart doeth good **like** a medicine: but a broken spirit drieth the bones.'"

"Did you memorize that just for me?"

"Actually, it was a memory verse in my first grade Sunday school class at Pastor Palmer's church. He's been the pastor at the First Methodist Church of Franklin for many, many years. In fact, he married my parents. My mother was pregnant with Carrie Emeline and me when she arrived here in Franklin."

Loretta looked at him with such confusion that he had to smile. "I think the cat got your tongue."

"Well, yes. Your mother touched on the story at my first dinner with your family at Christmas Hotel the day I arrived with Lydia Grace. She said she met your dad and Lily when she arrived in Franklin in December of nineteen forty-one. She said they married on New Year's Eve nineteen forty-one, and said you and Carrie Emeline were born the next year. I suppose I thought around October or November."

He looked at her nonchalantly, and she was quick to add, "Oh, please don't think I'm condemning your mother. Far from it!" She worried he might think her comment sounded critical.

Ken patted her hand. "I didn't think that. Here's the story. My mom and my dad were married to other people. Lily was born in 1936 to Christopher and Ellie Wright. My mother Jerilyn was twenty years old when she met Christopher in December, 1941. My mother was running away from her home, family, and friends. She received the telegram that my biological father Kenneth Seifert was killed at the bombing of Pearl Harbor.

"She boarded a train from Dayton, Ohio with the intentions of meeting some of her husband's family in Nashville, Tennessee. As my mother would say, 'The Lord had a different plan for her.' She was robbed of her purse when she switched trains in your hometown of Cincinnati."

Loretta wrinkled her nose at him.

"Sorry, but it's the truth. Mom didn't know her purse had been stolen until she arrived at the train stop here in Franklin, Kentucky. She thought it was the second worst day of her life; the first being the day the telegram arrived that informed her that her husband was dead. She was now widowed, pregnant, penniless, and a stranger in a small town. However, to make a long story short, she met Christopher and Lily, fell in love with them, and they fell in love with her. Her extreme depression ended when she rededicated her life to the Lord.

"On New Year's Eve she became the wife of Christopher Wright and the twenty-year-old adoptive mother to five-year-old Lily. Then in May, Carrie Emeline and I were born. Christopher became our father. I've never known a father other than Christopher, and Lily has never known another mother than Jerilyn. We are all just as close as if we all three were born with the same parents."

He paused when their food arrived, and he reached for Loretta's hand and asked a quick blessing on their food. She didn't protest his taking her hand, and listened to Ken's prayer.

As they ate, Loretta grew quiet again, and he smiled. "I suppose I've dominated the conversation. I think I'll shut up for a while and let you talk."

She finished chewing her bite of pork tenderloin. "Lately I've been thinking about how one incident can lead to another. Your parents' story is the perfect example. If Jerilyn's purse hadn't been stolen, she wouldn't have met Christopher. If I wasn't rooming with your sister

Lydia Grace, I wouldn't have been invited to Christmas Hotel. I would never have met you, your family, Cecilia, and Gloria. The path of life is strange. One incident can change the course of an entire life. When my parents died two and a half months ago, my whole life changed."

"Would you like to talk about it? I'm a good listener, and I don't judge."

"If I tell you *everything* about my life since my parents died, you'd probably make a quick exit."

"Try me," he challenged.

She put down her fork and wiped her mouth. "I'll tell you this part. My parents were driving to see me at UC when they were killed in a car crash by a drunk driver. They wouldn't have been coming, except I was considering quitting school and they wanted to talk me out of it. You see, if I hadn't thought about leaving UC, they wouldn't have been on the road that night. I'll have to carry the guilt of their deaths the rest of my life." She stopped talking and tried to eat another bite without choking up.

"You shouldn't feel guilty about something over which you had no control. Your parents were doing what any parent would do. Someday when you're a mother you'll understand."

She glanced at him as though he'd read her mind and knew she was pregnant. They continued to eat in silence. Finally, she looked straight into his eyes. "I'm not sure I ever want to be a mother. I've not been a very nice person since the death of my parents. I know your sister Lydia Grace would attest to that. I don't even know why Lydia Grace invited me here. She could have been free of my poor attitude for a couple of weeks, and she'd have enjoyed her Christmas vacation much more."

"Lydia Grace is a very loving individual. She's a good soul. She sees the best in people. She always has. I believe she saw who you are deep down, and also that you are hurting and wanted to be your friend. I can tell you're in pain, but I see good qualities about you, too, and I want to be your friend. Please know that if there's anything anyone in my family can help you with, you can ask any of us. We won't judge."

"Thank you, Ken. I'll keep that in mind."

"My dad will be preaching in Christmas Hotel's chapel on Christmas Eve and Christmas Day. Would you come and sit with me?"

"I'll keep that in mind, too." She looked at him and smiled. *I like him, and I don't want him to think I'm such a hardened person. Could I ever tell him about Barry and the frat party? I don't think so. No matter how much he likes me, what would he think of me if he knew?*

"I'll really consider your offer, Ken."

He returned the smile. "Thank you. Both services are wonderful. On Christmas Eve we have a candlelight service, which happens to fall on Sunday morning this year. It's also Lydia Grace's birthday, so she'll open her presents after the noon meal at Christmas Hotel. We'll also hold our Sunday evening service. On Monday morning, our family will open our Christmas gifts; have a special breakfast at home, and then head to the Christmas morning service. At all three services we'll sing Christmas hymns. Lily used to play for the services, until Lydia Grace became the accomplished pianist that she is. Lily and her family will be there on Christmas Day with her husband's parents. The Christmas Eve and Christmas services are a family tradition in the chapel at Christmas Hotel. Dad will read the Christmas story in Luke for the Christmas Eve service in the evening, and then the Christmas story in Matthew for the Christmas morning service."

Loretta listened politely, fidgeted in her seat, and said, "I really haven't been in the Christmas spirit lately."

"I'm sorry if I've overwhelmed you with all the events. You may feel differently and receive the Christmas spirit after all the services at Christmas Hotel. Many have. The offer still stands. If there's anyone in our family you'd like to talk with, all you need to do is ask."

"Thank you, Ken."

The waitress brought the check. Ken paid it, and escorted Loretta back to Christmas Hotel.

Chapter Twenty

A Picture is Worth a Thousand Words

"But we are all as an unclean thing, and all our righteousnesses are as filthy rags; and we all do fade as a leaf; and our iniquities, like the wind, have taken us away."
Isaiah 64:6

Thursday Evening, December 21, 1967
Loretta, Gloria, and Cecilia had not spent any time altogether since the Sunday morning church service. However, that evening they all wound up in the dining room of Christmas Hotel. The three arrived at the same time, and noticed the Wrights were not at their usual table. When Gloria asked their host where they should sit since the Wrights weren't there, she was told they were to use the Wrights' family table. He went on to explain that the Wrights were at home on South College Street having a family dinner, before Lily, John, and the four grandchildren returned to Russellville on Friday morning.

The girls were seated, and said nothing to each other as they checked the evening's selections. The waiter returned and took their orders. Their friendship had built last Friday and Saturday, but Gloria now sensed they were uncomfortable with each other. Finally, she broke the silence.

"You know, I hope that what happened to me at the service on Sunday doesn't harm the friendship that had begun between the three of us."

They just stared at her.

"I really want to be friends with both of you."

Neither girl responded. Their food arrived and Gloria said no more through the meal.

After the dishes were cleared from their table, she made another attempt, with a different approach. She silently prayed, *Lord Jesus, please help me to help them.* She took a deep breath. "Obviously, we all three have something in common. I don't know what it is, except we all visited Dr. Beasley's office, *and* on the same morning. I don't think that was a coincidence, so I'm going to tell you why I was there. I told Mrs. Wright on Sunday morning, when I went forward to the altar and rededicated my life to the Lord Jesus. Do you know what rededication means?"

Cecilia said, "Yes."

Loretta replied, "Not really."

Gloria addressed Loretta. "It means I'm a born again Christian – or saved, if you will – but I'd fallen away from the Lord. Sunday, I made things right with the Lord Jesus by the rededication of my life to Him."

The two continued to stare at her, but still didn't speak.

"Let me back up. When I found out my fiancé Matthew was MIA in Vietnam, I blamed God, and I said some pretty harsh things. I wanted nothing to do with God. I even told my parents I know longer wished to be a Christian. I was angry at God."

She stopped a moment and inhaled a big breath and exhaled it before continuing. "The night before Matthew left for Vietnam, he and I performed our own wedding service before God. We didn't have a minister present, but in our hearts, because God was there, we felt married. The Bible literally says that when two or more are gathered together, God is there. I'm not condoning what we did; I'm just stating the way we felt at the time. We consummated our illegal marriage that night. A few weeks later I suspected I might be pregnant. On December first the pregnancy was confirmed by a doctor, and on December eighth I found out Matthew was MIA."

Gloria had to stop, as a lump formed in her throat and her eyes filled with tears. She fumbled inside her purse looking for a tissue, and Loretta came to her rescue this time and handed her one. People began to glance over at their table with curious expressions.

"Let's go up to my room," suggested Cecilia.

"Thank you," said Gloria, as she wiped her eyes and dabbed at her nose.

When they were settled in Cecilia's room, Gloria continued. "I was so bitter. Before I left home, people everywhere I went kept asking how Matthew was faring in the army. Our close friends knew that he and I had been inseparable since birth. They were good, well-meaning people, and most were members of our church. Matthew's parents and my own are best friends, and as I told you before, they came here to Christmas Hotel for their joint honeymoons. It was hard to remain cordial to all the goodhearted people I encountered at home. Soon, they would know Matthew was MIA, *and* see I was pregnant. I couldn't stay there and answer their questions, and very soon what might be their condolences regarding Matthew. I knew I had to get away. That's when I made my decision to come here." She stopped and dabbed at her eyes. "I had actually considered an abortion."

Loretta spoke next. "I'm pregnant, too," she said, pointblank. "However, my baby wasn't conceived in love. My baby ... was conceived ... by a horrible experience." She stumbled on the statement. "I've not told anyone this story, but I want to tell you two. Not even Lydia Grace knows."

She stopped a second, glancing to each girl, and then continued. "I told you my parents died in a car crash. They were on their way to see me. I'd told them I was thinking about leaving school at the University of Cincinnati. I wasn't sure UC ... or any university was right for me. My parents were on their way to discuss the options with me when a drunk driver hit them head on. They died instantly." She grabbed a tissue, dabbed at her eyes, and blew her nose. "I'm sorry. I didn't mean to start crying."

"No need to be sorry," said Gloria softly.

"I told you that my brother Donald was able to fly home for the funeral. Unfortunately, we're not close. He's ten years older, and he's always away. The only thing we really had in common were our parents, and now that thread is severed. He's a lifer in the United States Air Force.

"Soon after the funeral, Donald returned to Germany, and I just wandered aimlessly through the days following. I blamed myself for the death of my parents. They wouldn't have been driving that night if it hadn't been for me. Like you, Gloria, I became bitter. During the week following my parents' death, I met Barry. He appeared to be compassionate about my loss. I had no one, so I clung to Barry and reveled in what I thought was possibly his love. However, I soon learned that it wasn't love. He was working his way into my life with completely dishonorable intentions. He knew how vulnerable I was.

"The weekend following the funeral, Barry invited me to a party at his fraternity house. Of course, I'd heard about the parties at that house, and I wasn't sure I should go, but I was lonely. I wanted companionship. I thought Barry might be different. That was the biggest mistake of my life. If my mom was still alive, I would have asked her advice. However, maybe because I blamed myself for her death, I made the terrible decision to go to the party." She looked at Gloria and Cecilia. "Do you really want to hear this?"

"Only if you want to tell it," said Gloria. "I certainly won't judge you."

"I'm on *your* side," said Cecilia. "I've had my share of bad boyfriends."

Loretta chuckled at that. "I can't imagine you've known *anyone* like Barry. I arrived at the frat house, and the party was in full swing. I have no idea where the house parents were, but they definitely weren't on the premises. I suppose they go home in the evening and leave the students in charge. I might be twenty-one, and three years older than you two, but I'm naïve ... or I *was*. The students were dancing to very loud music, and the alcohol was freely flowing. Marijuana was passed around. As soon as I walked in, I was handed a beer and a joint. I thought … why not? I felt so guilty about my parents' deaths, so why not get high and forget? I drank the beer and smoked the pot.

"As I got higher and higher, I saw a girl who appeared to be freaking out. Someone said she'd dropped acid. I didn't know what that meant. The girl was having hallucinations. She kept saying spiders were crawling on her. She was hitting herself all over her body. It was disturbing to watch. So when someone asked me if I wanted to take a trip like that girl, I just said 'no thank you.' I kept asking where Barry was. They'd shrug their shoulders like they didn't know.

"Finally, I saw Barry coming down from the upstairs with a pretty blonde. He walked up to me and asked if I'd like to take a trip to Heaven with him. I had no idea what he meant, and I'm sure he could tell I was confused. My beer was empty, so he thrust another into my hands. We sat together on a sofa and watched the people dancing. Periodically, some of the couples left the room and went upstairs."

Loretta looked at Cecilia and Gloria. "Are you sure you want to hear this? It gets much worse."

"I can handle it," said Cecilia.

"I may be a deacon's daughter, but I can handle it, too," said Gloria.

"Okay. Well, here's what happened," said Loretta clenching her jaw. "Barry lit another joint, and we smoked it together, while continuing to drink our beers. I'd never smoked pot or drank beer before. Barry began to kiss me, and I was dizzy and pretty much out of it. Barry asked me if I'd go upstairs with him. He said he wanted to talk to me in private." Loretta pursed her lips and smiled wryly. "Did I mention I was naïve?"

Gloria offered a sympathetic smile.

Loretta sighed and then continued. "I walked up the steps holding onto Barry with one hand and the banister with the other. I knew I was both drunk and high. I thought Barry would take care of me. After all, he was my friend ... right? He cared about me ... right? Wrong. We entered his room. He closed the door, and right away started taking off my clothes. I told him no, but he didn't stop. He said it would be all right, and that I shouldn't worry. He pushed me onto the bed, and continued to kiss me. I heard the door open, and at least three other guys walked in. Then I passed out."

Loretta paused and didn't say anything for a minute. "I don't know if it was just Barry, or if the others violated me, too. All I know is that I woke up the next morning, wrapped in a blanket, and lying on the downstairs sofa. My clothes were in a heap on the floor beside me. The room smelled of beer, stale cigarettes, and pot. People slept haphazardly on the floor. My head ached along with my body. I cried for my lost innocence. I cried for my parents. I cried for my brother. I wanted to die."

The tears now filled Loretta's eyes, but she continued. "Within five weeks, I knew I was pregnant. It's been confirmed. I'm considering an abortion if I can find a clinic to have it done. I don't want to carry a baby from a rapist ... or rapists. I used to be a nice person, but I know I've changed. I don't know how Lydia Grace puts up with me as her roommate, and why she even invited me here. My other roommate walked out on me. I can't say I blame her. My attitude has become surly and bitter. I'm sure you two have noticed," and she laughed in a cynical way.

Cecilia waited a moment before she spoke. "I *was* pregnant," she said, "but I had an abortion about three weeks ago, on December first to be exact." She waited to view Gloria and Loretta's expressions, but there was no condemnation. "I come from a wonderful Christian family in Houston. I have two younger brothers, whom I adore. I never got saved, but I understand salvation. I'm the rebellious child, the black sheep of the family. I wanted nothing to do with church. I skipped church whenever possible. I know my parents saw through my pretend illnesses.

"My boyfriend Ernie planned our escape to freedom on our high school graduation day, June fourth. We had the saddlebags packed on his Harley Davidson motorcycle, and left straight after the graduation ceremony. It was a Sunday, and in my room I left my parents the note saying I was leaving, I didn't know when I would return, and not to look for me. I was eighteen, so they couldn't have me reported a runaway. Ernie and I wanted the choice to do as we pleased. The only problem was Ernie. I thought he loved me." She looked straight at Loretta. "You'll see, he was as rotten a boyfriend as Barry.

"We'd heard about all the college students heading to the Haight-Asbury district of San Francisco. It's now deemed the summer of love. I'd *hardly* call what went on there as love," she muttered in a bitter tone.

"Everywhere we went, we saw other young people, just as rebellious as we were. I look back now, and I call it the summer of selfishness. We were enjoying our independence from obligations and family. I was doing everything that would leave my Christian parents heartbroken, if they knew.

"Ernie and I rented a cheap and dirty one-room apartment with our meager funds. I discovered that Ernie had a hot temper when he was stoned. I remember some Bible verses about a hot-tempered man. 'Make no friendship with an angry man; and with a furious man thou shalt not go: Lest thou learn his ways, and get a snare to thy soul.'"

Gloria nodded. "That's in the book of Proverbs," she said. "I think it's in chapter twenty-two."

"It might be," Cecilia said. "It's one of those Bible verses that seemed to stick in my mind. I think it means if you associate with people who keep losing their temper, you become like them. When I confronted Ernie about his affairs with other women in the district, he slapped me and told me to mind my own business.

"At the end of the summer I walked away from him and hitched a ride with another couple headed to Chicago. They left me in Omaha, Nebraska. From there I hitched a ride to Dallas, and then another ride to my friend Donna's apartment in Houston. Donna was the one who told me where I could go to get the abortion. The kind taxi driver who drove me to the abortionist is a Christian. He tried to talk me out of the abortion. I didn't listen.

"Afterwards, he and his wife helped me find a reputable doctor to treat me. The doctor even gave me a pamphlet about the growth of the fetus, but I've never looked at it. He also lectured me about the abortion and my future pregnancies." Cecilia rummaged in her purse, and buried near the bottom she pulled out the wrinkled and torn pamphlet. "I was only around three months pregnant, and my friend Donna told me it wasn't a baby yet; therefore, it was okay to have an abortion." Cecilia opened the pamphlet.

Gloria reached in her purse, pulling out the picture Dr. Beasley gave her. Loretta fished around in her purse for what Gloria assumed to be the same thing since she'd also been to see Dr. Beasley. They both pulled the pictures free at the same time.

Gloria smiled when she looked at her picture. When she turned to Loretta, she recognized the disbelief on her face. Cecilia's expression was not only one of disbelief, but also horror, and then pain.

Finally Gloria spoke. "I've decided to carry my baby to term. I no longer want an abortion, especially after Dr. Beasley gave me this picture. I still don't know if I'll keep the baby or give it up for adoption, but I definitely will *not* abort Matthew's baby."

Loretta and Cecilia still stared at their pictures, neither speaking. Curious, Loretta and Gloria peeked over Cecilia's shoulder. Her pamphlet included all the stages of development of the unborn child.

After a couple minutes of silence, Gloria asked, "Would you two like to talk about the pictures?"

Loretta took a deep breath and answered. "I

considered abortion, but now I see I'm carrying a baby. There's no denying that this is a picture of a miniature child. How can anyone say this is a blob of tissue and plasma? I'm about ten weeks pregnant, and I'm seeing complete body parts, just small. I'm angry about the lies I've been told! Dr. Beasley was the only one who told me the truth." She stopped a minute to catch her breath and then turned to Gloria. "This baby wasn't conceived in love like your baby, Gloria, but I can't take the life of an innocent child. It's not the baby's fault how he or she was conceived. If I abort the baby, then the baby and I are both victims of Barry and possibly his friends, and that's not fair to the baby."

Cecilia remained quiet. Gloria watched the tear slide down her cheek, but she said nothing as Cecilia wiped it away. Gloria asked, "Cecilia, do you want to talk about what you see?"

"No, I don't," Cecilia said in a hoarse voice. "I just want to be left alone. Please leave ... both of you."

Gloria and Loretta rose. "If you decide you want to talk about the abortion or anything, at any time in the night, please just knock on my door," said Gloria. "I'll be here for you, and for you, too, Loretta. Also, remember Mr. Wright is a pastor for Christmas Hotel's chapel. I think we all should speak with him. I may have rededicated my life to

Jesus Christ, but I still hurt regarding Matthew. It's so difficult."

They left and closed the door, leaving Cecilia sitting on her bed, still staring at the pamphlet.

Chapter Twenty-One

The Bent-Over Woman

*"And, behold, there was a woman which had a
spirit of infirmity eighteen years, and was bowed
together, and could in no wise lift up herself."*
Luke 13: 11

Friday, December 22, 1967
It was six o'clock in the morning, and Loretta was
outside Christmas Hotel furiously shoveling snow.
Lydia Grace appeared, because Chris called her and
told her what was happening.

"What are you doing out here, Loretta? We have
staff to do this," said Lydia Grace in a gentle but
firm voice.

"I'm trying to work off some anger. I didn't
sleep well last night."

"What are you angry about?"

"Why should you care, Lydia Grace! I've been
nothing but unkind toward you. You wouldn't
understand anyway. You wouldn't understand pain

and suffering."

"Please put the shovel down, Loretta. I think it's time for us to have a long overdue talk. Room number seven is kept reserved for my family, and that's where we should go. I have a story to tell you."

"Okay." Loretta grudgingly propped the shovel against the building and followed Lydia Grace into the lobby. As they knocked the snow off their boots, they overheard Eugene speaking to Chris.

"I've tried to talk to Cecilia, but she won't answer my knocks at her door. When I knocked, I said who I was, but still no response. I heard her stirring around in her room an hour ago, so I know she's awake. Did she tell you no calls, Chris?"

"Well, yes, indirectly. She told Mr. Mullins late last night, while he had desk duty. Maybe she doesn't want to be bothered, so you should give her some privacy this morning."

"Okay. I'm going to have breakfast in the dining room. Please come and get me if she calls down to you or you see her."

"I will."

Lydia Grace waited until Eugene walked away and then stepped up to the front desk. "I'd like the key to our family room please, Chris. Loretta and I will be in there for a while, so I'll put out the do-not-disturb sign."

"Certainly, Sis," he said, as he handed her the key.

Loretta followed Lydia Grace up the staircase. Lydia Grace unlocked the door, put out the do-not-disturb sign, opened the nightstand drawer, retrieved some matches, and lit the kerosene lamp on the table by the door. After Loretta was in the room, Lydia Grace locked the door from the inside. "Wow! This room looks like it's in a time warp!" said Loretta in awe.

Loretta absorbed the beauty of the nineteenth century room with an obvious expression of amazement. Her eyes scanned the room. Aligning two of the walls, she saw a high four-poster oak bed, a marble top oak dresser with an attached matching mirror, a ladies vanity on which lay a silver tray holding an antique mother of pearl hairbrush, comb, and hand mirror. A second kerosene lamp sat on the table between two brocade chairs in front of a window. Lydia Grace leaned over and lit the second lamp and sat down on one of the chairs. Heavy deep green velvet drapes pooled on the floor from four floor-to-ceiling windows. Centered between the four windows, a set of french doors led to a small balcony. A writing desk with very small drawers and pigeon holes stood against another wall.

"In a way, that's true," said Lydia Grace.

"Christmas Hotel was built in eighteen-fifty by Thomas Hoy and his wife Lucy Goodnight Hoy. They were a prominent couple in Franklin at the time. They wanted to build the hotel so people could come here and experience the birth of Jesus every day. In eighteen eighty-three, Captain Jacob Barnabas Bazell and his wife Mary Eve Winters Bazell arrived here with the intent to purchase Christmas Hotel. They brought their twenty-year-old daughter, Carrie Emeline."

"That's the name of your sister."

"Yes, and my sister was named for her. This room was where their daughter Carrie Emeline stayed when the Bazells first arrived eighty-four years ago. Captain and Mrs. Bazell stayed in room number eight, where Cecilia is right now. After their daughter died of pneumonia the following March, Mr. and Mrs. Bazell decided not to change the décor of this one particular room. It became the untouched room at Christmas Hotel: that is until my mother arrived in December of 1941. There was no room at the inn, you might say. The Bazells gave her this room which had not been used since their daughter died."

Lydia Grace stopped to allow this information to register with Loretta. "Please have a seat, Loretta, on this chair." She pointed to the other brocade chair.

Loretta complied. "Ken told me the story about your mom's arrival in Franklin, when we had lunch on Wednesday."

"Good. I'm glad he did. "

"I can relate somewhat to your mom," said Loretta. "I'm not widowed or penniless, but I feel her depression. I'm pregnant."

Lydia Grace carefully controlled her expression, so as to not show shock; just compassion. She didn't want Loretta to feel as if she was being judged. She knew there was more to Loretta's story than the death of her parents.

Loretta continued after a short pause. "I didn't want to carry the baby ... until now. You see ... I was raped." Loretta broke down and began to cry.

Lydia Grace felt the pain and trauma Loretta must have felt. Tears welled in her own eyes when she rose and grabbed a box of tissues off the night stand. She knelt on the floor in front of Loretta, handing her the box. When Lydia Grace was finally able to speak, it was in a soft and caring voice, "You remind me of a lady in the book of Luke in the Bible. She was a woman who was bent over, carrying a burden. I believe you've been carrying a burden, Loretta, and for much too long. It's time to release your burden."

After Loretta composed herself, she said, "I was in Dr. Beasley's office and he gave me a picture of what my baby looks like now. My baby is small, but every part of his or her body is the same as a newborn baby; the same as Lily's six month old baby Ellie. I considered abortion. I was told it was just a blob of plasma, or a fish. In the picture I saw a baby. Very small, but a baby. I was either misinformed or deliberately lied to.

"The rape happened six days after my parents died in that terrible car accident. I've been bitter, stupid, and angry. I know I haven't been very pleasant to be around. I couldn't talk to you. You're so perfect. Everyone likes you, and you're happy and cheerful all the time. How can someone like you understand pain, sorrow, and evil? You were born with the proverbial silver spoon in your mouth."

Lydia Grace still knelt on the floor in front of Loretta. She took Loretta's hands in hers. Drawing a deep breath she slowly expelled the air. "You're wrong about me, Loretta. Let me tell you about the first eight years of my life. I was born at the hospital in Nashville on Christmas Eve, 1946. The next morning I was kidnapped from my room by a staff nurse."

Loretta's countenance changed from a look of bitterness to one of deep felt sorrow. Lydia Grace stood and sat back again on the brocade chair.

"I overheard your mom tell a lady named Carol

Ann in Dr. Beasley's waiting room that you were kidnapped at birth. I didn't know you were gone for eight years. I'm sorry."

"The kidnapper's name was Rose Clark, and she was in a deep depression from the death of her beloved husband on Thanksgiving Day, *and* her newborn daughter Lucille Grace on December third. She didn't think about what she was doing. She just reacted and stole me. She immediately left Nashville with me, and we moved to live in an apartment across the hall from her sister Eula Mae and Eula Mae's husband Otto Smith, and their four children in Bowling Green, Kentucky. I thought their children were my cousins, and the Smiths knew no different. They really thought I was Rose Clark's daughter, whom she called Lucy."

Loretta's widened eyes and her steady gaze told Lydia Grace that her friend listened closely. "Loretta, I really want you to know my story. Okay?"

"Okay," said Loretta.

"My life changed on December first, 1954 when Mama Rose died. On the same day, Eula Mae and Otto threw me out into the cold with nothing but a thin dress, a threadbare coat and worn out shoes. I prayed to the Baby Jesus in the Nativity manger at the church Mama Rose and I attended. I told Jesus I was cold, scared, alone, and my mama was dead. I told Him that it was also my eighth birthday, or the birthday I thought was mine. I wrapped my coat around me, and I fell asleep under some bushes near the fountain in the square in Bowling Green. I awakened in the night, very cold. A big dog lay down by me and kept me warm. I called the dog Bullet.

"In the morning, I met an old man named Mr. Gabe who took the dog and me to Christmas Hotel. His intentions were for the Wrights to find me a home. However, the Smiths had other thoughts. They smelled money and came for me, demanding I be returned to them."

"I'm so sorry, Lydia Grace. It must have been awful."

"It was, but good things came of it. After eight years I was returned to my true parents: the Wrights. The four children I thought were my cousins were adopted by Darius and Barbara Scott, who are a fine family. You met them and their four children at the McLemore farm. I'm telling you this, so you'll know my life hasn't always been as you envisioned. I was *not* born with a silver spoon in my mouth. In fact, I lived the first eight years of my life in a slum apartment. Mama Rose was good to me, but she just wasn't my real mom. I lost out on what the first eight years of my life should have been."

"You don't appear bitter at all."

Lydia Grace smiled. "I won't lie to you. I was at first. When my mom and my dad told me my true identity, I was angry at Rose Clark. I was angry she stole me. My parents helped me to forgive Mama Rose. That's what we call her when we refer to her. Mama Rose was a good woman deep down; just a very troubled, depressed, and confused woman.

"Once I forgave Mama Rose, I was then able to concentrate on Jesus. My parents, my sisters, and my older brother knew Jesus, so I wanted Him in my heart, too. Although I was only eight, I understood sin. I knew that I wasn't a perfect little girl. I didn't have huge sins, but I knew that at times I told lies, and that was wrong. I'd been to Sunday school with Mama Rose, and I knew the Bible said the wages of sin is death. That meant when I died I would *not* go to Heaven with Jesus, but that I'd go to Hell with Satan. That scared me. I felt the conviction in my young heart. My dad asked me if I wanted Jesus to save my soul, and I said I did."

Lydia Grace rose, retrieved the Bible from the drawer in the night stand, and showed Loretta where to find particular verses in the Bible.

"I think you would probably like to get revenge on your attacker. Am I right, Loretta?"

"Yes, I would."

She flipped through the Bible. "Well, the Bible says in Romans chapter twelve and verse nineteen, 'Dearly beloved, avenge not yourselves, but rather give place unto wrath: for it is written, Vengeance *is* mine; I will repay, saith the Lord.' In other words, the Lord will take care of the person who hurt you, much better than you can. You just need to trust in the Lord.

"Loretta, if you hold onto your anger, your anger will hold on to you. Would you like Jesus to save your soul? Do you want redemption? Do you feel a tug on your heart, that the Lord has you under conviction?"

Lydia Grace could tell by Loretta's sorrowful eyes and puckered lips that she was in deep thought, and then she began to cry again. At last Loretta answered with a firm response. "Yes, I feel the tug. I just didn't know what it was. I need redemption. I don't want to go to Hell. I want what you have. I want to be happy again. I want a new life. I want to be rid of my old life. You're right. I've been carrying a burden. I want this burden gone."

"He'll change your life, Loretta. You need to believe that He'll forgive you, that He died for your sin, and be sure that you're willing to turn from your past life. Ask Him to come into your heart. He died on the cross, so that all who believed in Him would be forgiven of their sins, and would live with

Him eternally. He paid our sin debt for us by dying on the cross. Would you now like to pray and ask Him to save you, Loretta?"

Loretta nodded. "Yes."

"Take my hands. He's with us now. Just talk to Him from your heart."

For more than a minute Loretta remained silent. Lydia Grace was not going to coax or encourage her. It was up to Loretta now.

Eventually Loretta spoke through her tears. "Dear Lord Jesus, I've been a sinner. Even though my parents died, I knew I shouldn't have gone to that party. I've been unkind and bitter. I don't blame You for the death of my parents, or for the rape. It wasn't Your fault. I know there are evil people in the world. Lydia Grace doesn't blame You for the evil that happened to her, and I won't either."

She paused, and then continued in a hoarse voice. "I'm sorry for the thoughts I had about this baby. It's not the baby's fault. I won't take the life of the baby. I know You died for my sin. I want to turn from my sin. I'll need Your help. I ask You to come into my heart and life. I want to live in Heaven with You, Jesus, when my time comes. Thank You for saving me. Amen."

Lydia Grace echoed her amen and hugged Loretta. "Loretta, that was honest and beautiful.

You are now my sister in Christ, and I love you."

"I love you, too, Lydia Grace. I'm sorry I was so nasty to you."

"Well, that's past. I hope we'll always be friends, for the rest of our lives."

"I hope so, too."

"How do you feel right now?"

"I feel calm and at peace."

A loud crash shattered the stillness of the mood. Both girls jumped and ran to the door. "I think it came from Cecilia's room," said Loretta.

Lydia Grace unlocked and flung open the door and both girls ran next door to check.

"Cecilia!" yelled Lydia Grace as she pounded on the door.

Gloria opened the door of her room. "I heard the commotion. What happened?" she asked.

"I don't know, but I think the noise came from Cecilia's room," said Lydia Grace. "She's not answering the door. Please go get Chris for the key. Tell him it's an emergency!"

Gloria ran down the stairs. Chris and Eugene stood at the front desk. "We need the key to Cecilia's room. We heard a crash, and she's not answering our knock."

Chris grabbed the key, and Eugene was already bounding up the steps two at a time with Chris following right behind him. When they entered the room, Cecilia lay in a crumbled heap on the floor.

"She must have fallen into the nightstand, because the phone and lamp are both on the floor with her," said Lydia Grace.

Eugene tried to shake her awake and patted her cheeks, with no result.

"Her body is warm," said Eugene. He felt her pulse in her wrist and then her carotid artery. "Her pulse is weak."

"There's a water glass and pill bottle still on the night stand." Loretta picked up the bottle. "It's nearly empty. She must have taken these sleeping pills, but I don't know how many. It says on the bottle it held a hundred."

"I know how many," said Gloria. "I literally ran into her at the drug store when she was leaving. The bottle fell onto the sidewalk from the sack she was holding. It was a new bottle. She'd just purchased it."

"We've got to get her to Dr. Beasley," said Eugene, taking charge. "Hand me the quilt from her bed."

Lydia Grace did as he asked, and Eugene wrapped Cecilia in it. "I'm going to carry her to Dr. Beasley's office. You girls can follow me with the pill bottle. Chris, you call Dr. Beasley and tell him we're on our way, and what to expect."

Within seconds they were down the stairs and

out the door. Eugene ran as fast as he could, carrying Cecilia's dead weight. When they entered Dr. Beasley's office the doctor was ready for them.

"Lay her on this table, and then step out to the waiting room," he commanded.

The friends obeyed ... and waited.

Chapter Twenty-Two

The Long Day and Night

*"Brethren, if any of you do err from the
truth, and one convert him: Let him know,
that he which converteth the sinner from the
error of his way shall save a soul from death,
and shall hide a multitude of sins."*
James 5: 19-20

Friday, December 22, through
Saturday morning, December 23, 1967
Two hours later, Dr. Beasley walked into the
waiting room with his first report. Christopher,
Jerilyn, Ken, and Carrie Emeline had joined
Eugene, Lydia Grace, Loretta, and Gloria. They
were holding hands, and Eugene was leading the
group in prayer when Dr. Beasley entered. "Amen,"
said Eugene and the others responded in kind.

Eugene raised his head and saw Dr. Beasley.
"How is she?" he inquired.

"I've pumped Cecilia's stomach, and she's
resting. Because she was unconscious, I had to

insert an endotracheal tube through her nose before I could pump her stomach. This tube protects the airway, and prevents Cecilia from breathing the stomach fluids into the lungs. Then I inserted a lubricated stomach tube through her mouth, into the esophagus, and down to the stomach. I was able to suction out the contents of her stomach through the tube."

Dr. Beasley paused, and regarded the group of family and friends. "Should I continue?"

Eugene knew Dr. Beasley was worried about how much he should reveal, so Eugene responded for the group, "Please continue, Dr. Beasley."

The four young ladies and Jerilyn looked down at the floor, and Eugene surmised that he might have spoken too soon, and they may not wish to visualize the whole process in such detail. He decided to be certain they wanted to stay by asking them. They agreed to stay, and he then nodded to Dr. Beasley to continue.

"Okay," Dr. Beasley said. "Nurse Wilson and I washed out Cecilia's stomach with salt water. The stomach is now clear. We administered activated charcoal. The charcoal absorbs any drugs that may still be in the stomach. The activated charcoal was given with a cathartic, which is a medication that speeds the emptying of the intestines."

"Is she conscious?" asked Eugene, which was

the main information he wanted.

"Not at this time. Forty percent of people in a comatose state are in the coma from the results of drug poisoning. It's a good thing you got her here when you did, while I could still pump her stomach. If forty-five more minutes had lapsed, most likely *all* the poison would have been absorbed into her bloodstream."

"What's the next step?" asked Christopher.

"I need to keep her here at least until tomorrow morning for observation. She's not out of the woods. The charcoal only absorbs what was in the stomach. I still don't know what may be in her bloodstream. I'm hoping she didn't take a large quantity earlier, stop, and take more just before you found her. We'll know more by morning. I'm sending material from her stomach to the lab for analysis. The results may determine whether an antidote is needed, or if Cecilia should be monitored longer. When she awakens, she will need to be counseled to make sure it's safe to leave her alone."

"What happens after she's able to go to our home, or back to her room?" asked Lydia Grace.

"When a counselor feels Cecilia's mind is stable enough to leave from my clinic, she may have problems such as a sore throat for a day or two, and possible nose bleeds because of the tube. She could begin vomiting, which can lead to aspiration. That's breathing in the contents of the stomach. This can cause aspiration pneumonia."

"Can we go in and see her?" asked Eugene.

"I don't see why not," said Dr. Beasley. "I can move her to my largest room. A suicide patient needs to know she's cared about and loved. It will aid in her mental evaluation and her recovery."

"May we talk to her and read to her?" asked Gloria. "I thought if we let her know how much we cared, and read the Bible to her, it would help."

Dr. Beasley smiled, "You're on the right track, young lady. That's exactly what Cecilia needs."

"Would it be okay if I bring my violin and flute, and we sing hymns to her?" asked Lydia Grace. "Would it disturb your other patients?"

"I think my patients would enjoy the music and the singing. I'll just turn that old elevator music off. I don't much care for it anyway. Let me get her moved, and I'll be back for the ..." Dr. Beasley stopped, as he did a quick count. "... eight of you. That should be enough people to show Cecilia she's loved. They say the unconscious can hear."

"Jerilyn and I can attest to that," said Christopher. "If you remember, Dr. Beasley, when Lily was five she was hit by a car. Because of the head trauma, we had to take her to the hospital in Nashville. When she awakened, she remembered the words of love Jerilyn and I spoke to her."

Dr. Beasley nodded, "I remember it well, Christopher."

"When Lily awakened from the coma, she told us many things we said to her while she was unconscious, and could remember the Scripture reading, and the songs we sang. I know Cecilia will be able to hear us."

Lydia Grace dashed home and quickly returned with her violin and flute. She unpacked the violin from its case, placed it under her chin and on her left shoulder, and began to play "Rock of Ages" while the others sang. Eugene held Cecilia's hand. After several hymns, Lydia Grace placed her violin back in the case and picked up her flute.

"I'm so amazed that you play the piano, organ, violin, *and* the flute," said Loretta in wonder. "I didn't know that."

Ken added. "*Plus* the harp, guitar, bass fiddle, sax, and the clarinet!"

Loretta's eyes widened. "Wow, you're a one-woman orchestra!"

Lydia Grace smiled and played "Silent Night" with her flute.

"I've never heard it played more beautifully," said Gloria, as she wiped a tear from her eye. Loretta wiped tears from her eyes, too.

Christopher began to look for Bible passages to

read to Cecilia.

"I have a chapter in Psalms that means a lot to me," said Eugene. "If you don't mind, sir, I'd like to read part of it to Cecilia, and then tell her what it means to me."

Christopher handed Eugene his Bible. Eugene flipped to the middle of the Bible and found Psalms chapter ninety-one, and began to read the first few verses while holding Cecilia's hand.

"'He that dwelleth in the secret place of the most High shall abide under the shadow of the Almighty. I will say of the Lord, He is my refuge and my fortress: my God; in him will I trust. Surely he shall deliver thee from the snare of the fowler, and from the noisome pestilence.'"

Eugene paused, took a breath, and said to the unconscious Cecilia. "I want you to know what these verses in Psalms mean to me. You know that my biological parents were cruel. I told you the story. When Darius and Barbara Scott adopted me, I became a voracious Bible reader. I needed to know everything God expected of me, and I wanted to trust Him. I didn't understand salvation. The Scotts took the four of us to church, and I heard the Word preached, but I needed to bury it in my heart. I still held the pain and suffering of growing up with Otto and Eula Mae. Keep in mind that I was fourteen, nearly a man when I was adopted.

"I read this Psalm and felt as though I'd been in the secret place of the Almighty God. He had been keeping His arm around me all those years. I knew that He was my refuge and fortress, and I could trust Him. I saw the deliverance from the fowler like the danger of Otto and Eula Mae. He delivered me from the repulsive virus that was Otto and Eula Mae. I knew that He would cover me with His truth, so I would no longer be troubled with night terrors or the dangers of the day.

"I know that He will tread on any dangers that come my way. He has loved me, delivered me, and He even knew my name. He was my redeemer. The Lord Jesus wants to be your redeemer, too, Cecilia.

"I was fifteen before I received the Lord Jesus as my Savior. I had to learn how to trust. Lastly, I was waiting for Him to call upon me to use me in a troubled situation. I'm here today for you, Cecilia, because I care very much about you, and I want to honor Him. I pray all of this for you, and for you to wake up. There are eight of us here who care very much. I don't know what's troubling you, Cecilia, but I hope you'll tell me soon. Let all of us help. We will never judge you."

While Eugene spoke to Cecilia, Ken took Loretta's hand and she used a tissue to wipe her eyes with the other hand. When Eugene finished, Lydia Grace picked up the flute and played

"Amazing Grace."

All through the night, while Cecilia remained in the coma, Eugene, Loretta, Ken, Gloria, and Lydia Grace prayed, read the Bible, and sang. Christopher, Jerilyn, and Carrie Emeline left for home around eleven that night, and called Chris with an update just as he was leaving Christmas Hotel.

Eugene never stopped holding Cecilia's hand. Ken did the same with Loretta. Dr. Beasley and Nurse Wilson arrived twice in the night, but each time shook their heads and sadly reported they saw no change.

*****

At four o'clock, Loretta asked Ken to take a walk with her. They settled on a sofa in the waiting room. "I have something I want to tell you," said Loretta. "Yesterday morning, before this happened with Cecilia, Lydia Grace led me to the Lord."

"That's wonderful, Loretta! I'm so happy for you," he said and hugged her.

She smiled. "There's more that I want you to know ... I need you to know. The night before, Cecilia, Gloria, and I were together in Cecilia's room. We all made a confession to each other. We'd all been to see Dr. Beasley. I'm just going to say it outright. You'll soon know anyway. Gloria and I are pregnant." She waited for a look of horror or any look of disgust from Ken, but saw none.

He squeezed her hand in support. "Remember, I said my family and I don't judge. You can tell me anything."

Loretta took a deep breath. "Gloria and I had both considered abortions, but Gloria decided she wouldn't do that after she rededicated her life to Jesus, although she hasn't ruled out adoption for her baby. Dr. Beasley gave both of us pictures of what our babies look like at approximately ten weeks. I was certain I was going to have an abortion – until I saw the picture. You see … I'm pregnant … because I was raped."

This time his expression changed. He looked stunned. "Loretta, I'm so sorry. I can't imagine the pain you've suffered. No wonder you said you've been bitter and unkind."

"I need to finish," Loretta said as she placed her hand on his arm to stop him. "I don't want to start crying again before I tell you everything." She relayed the events of that night, as she told them to Gloria and Cecilia. "I trusted Barry. I was so wrong about him. I want to trust a man again, but I'm scared. Now that I'm a Christian, I'm going to trust God to help me heal. I need to heal from the death of my parents, *and* from the rape. The Bible verses Eugene read tonight for Cecilia, and then interpreted what the verses meant to him, really touched my heart."

"I hope you'll learn to trust *me*, too, Loretta. I want to know you better. I'm not at all like Barry and his friends. Whether you decide to keep the baby or give the child up for adoption won't change my growing feelings for you."

"How can you possibly have growing feelings for me? I've been awful."

"I saw inside you, to the real Loretta the first day I met you at the McLemore farm. It wasn't your beauty either, although I can't help from finding you attractive." He smiled. "Good things come in small packages, you know."

That broke the tension, and they were able to laugh together.

He continued. "So, Dr. Beasley gave you a picture of a ten-week baby in the womb. What does it look like?"

"I have it in my purse." She reached in, unfolded the picture, and handed it to Ken.

"Wow! This is amazing. It really *is* a baby ... just small."

"That's what I said, too. In fact, Cecilia had a whole pamphlet on the growth of the baby. I knew when I saw this picture, that I couldn't abort the baby. It's not the baby's fault he or she was conceived in rape. But I'm not sure at this stage of my life, and because the baby was conceived by rape, I could be a good mother. However, I'm definitely leaning toward adoption. I want to finish school, and I want the baby placed in a loving home."

"Speaking of school ... do you really want to return to UC after what happened?"

"No, I don't. I'll need to transfer to another college."

"I know just where you should transfer, if you're willing. I'd very much like to get to know you better. I need to return to UK on January second. Would you consider moving to Lexington and transferring to UK?"

Loretta smiled. "After all I just told you, you'd want me to move to Lexington?"

He didn't hesitate, "Yes. You can get an apartment, or live in the girls' dorm." He must have read the expression on her face, because he said, "Don't worry ... I'm not asking you to live with me."

She smiled at him. "I know you weren't thinking that. I wouldn't anyway. I can't move immediately. I need to work with the attorney and get my parents' estate closed. I'll probably want to sell their home. I see no reason to hang on to it ... especially when I'm living in Lexington, Kentucky."

"So ... that means you'll come?" he asked, sounding hopeful.

"Yes, I'll come. The baby will be born in July, so

I can register for the fall quarter next year." Then she studied his face. "What if you and I don't work out? We really don't know each other that well."

"That's true, but if we don't try, we'll always wonder. I want to try."

"Thank you for caring, Ken. I want to try, too."

"You're quite welcome. By the way, why was Cecilia at Dr. Beasley's office? Is she pregnant, too?"

"I'll let her tell that story when she awakens."

*****

Ken and Loretta returned to the room at five-thirty. Gloria and Lydia Grace had fallen asleep in their chairs, but Eugene was still awake, holding Cecilia's hand.

"Any change?" asked Loretta softly, so as not to awaken the girls.

"I'm afraid not," said Eugene.

Cecilia stirred, just slightly.

"Look, she moved her hand," said Eugene.

"I see it!" said Loretta in excitement.

Dr. Beasley and Nurse Wilson entered, and Loretta bumped Gloria and Lydia Grace in her excitement. Everyone was now awake to hear the good news.

"How's the patient?" asked Dr. Beasley.

"She just moved her hand," said Eugene.

Dr. Beasley opened each of Cecilia's eyelids and

shined the light. "She's waking up," he said.

Loretta smiled through tears when Cecilia moved her head toward Eugene, and her eyes fluttered. She finally opened them and looked straight at Eugene. He bent over and hugged her.

"Welcome back, Cecilia. We all missed you," he said, as his hand swept toward the others.

Cecilia tried to focus her eyes. "My ... throat ... hurts," she managed to say in a hoarse voice.

"It may hurt for a couple of days, Cecilia," Dr. Beasley explained. "Do you remember what happened?"

She licked her lips. "May I have some water?"

"I can't give you water yet, but you can suck on some ice cubes."

He had no sooner said that, when Nurse Wilson produced a cup filled with the ice cubes. She rubbed a cube on Cecilia's lips, and then placed it in Cecilia's mouth to dissolve.

"Thank ... you," said Cecilia in a slow whisper.

While Nurse Wilson checked Cecilia's vitals, Dr. Beasley again asked, "Do you remember what happened?"

"I took ... pills."

"Yes, you did. Your friends saved you."

While Cecilia looked around at all the anxious faces, Gloria stepped forward. "We all love and care about you, Cecilia. We were worried about you."

"How … can you … love me? You know what … I did to the baby," she said in a raspy voice.

Loretta stepped forward. "You only did what Gloria and I might have done."

"I can't forgive … myself."

Cecilia saw Christopher, Jerilyn, and Carrie Emeline standing in the hallway.

Dr. Beasley turned to them and said, "Please come in, and Nurse Wilson and I will step out. She needs all of you now – and the Lord."

Christopher walked up to her with Jerilyn at his side. "Why do you need to forgive yourself, Cecilia? If you'll tell me, I won't judge you. None of us will judge you."

Cecilia looked at all the faces and began to cry. She lifted her arm and swiped at the tears. Gloria handed her a tissue from the nightstand.

"I was … lied to. I believed … the lie … without checking … for the truth. I thought I was … was smarter than that." She dabbed her cheeks as tears spilled down her face. She stared into Eugene's eyes. "I was pregnant … pregnant, and I aborted … the baby … three weeks ago. When I saw … the picture of a three-months old … baby in the womb I … I was scared and … ashamed. I can't forgive … forgive myself."

"You can forgive yourself with the help of the Lord Jesus," said Eugene. "He's ready to forgive you your sins in the past, and your sins in the future. All you need to do is believe that He died on the cross to pay your sin debt. Do you know about salvation, Cecilia?"

"Yes. I've gone to ... to church all ... all my life. I know about ... Jesus. I was rebellious ... and I never got saved. Every time He knocked ... I walked out ... the church door. My parents ... are Christians, and so are ... my two little brothers." She looked at Gloria and Loretta. "Do they know ... know about you two?"

"Yes, they know everything," said Loretta.

"*You* can be ... be forgiven Loretta. It wasn't your fault. Gloria, *your* baby ... was conceived in love. I was just ... just plain foolish. I can't be ... forgiven."

"That doesn't matter," said Christopher, as he flipped through his Bible.

"May I have your Bible, Christopher?" asked Eugene. Christopher handed him the Bible, and Eugene quickly flipped through the pages. "Romans chapter ten and verses nine to eleven says that, 'If thou shalt confess with thy mouth the Lord Jesus, and shalt believe in thine heart that God hath raised him from the dead, thou shalt be saved. "

Cecilia continued to cry.

"Are you ready to be forgiven, Cecilia?" asked Eugene. "Are you ready to ask Jesus Christ to save you? Do you want His redemption? "

"Yes to all ... your questions."

He took her hands. "Cecilia, you've gone to church all of your life. You know what to do. From your heart, just ask Him."

She closed her eyes and was quiet for a moment. The tears ran down the sides of her face and into her ears. When she finally spoke, her voice was hoarse and halting. "Dear Heavenly ... Father, I've sinned ... and I'm sorry. I rebelled ... against the wonderful ... parents You gave me." She stopped and emitted a sob. "I know that ... my little brothers' hearts ... are probably broken ... over my actions." She stopped to catch her breath. "Please know that ... that I didn't know what ... I was doing ... regarding the baby. My behavior ... has been foolish. I know that if ... if I ask You, You will ... will come into my heart ... and into my life and save ... save me from my sins. I'm asking You, Jesus ... to redeem me. I need You." She sobbed again and began to cry harder. "Thank You, Jesus ... for saving me. I love ... You, Jesus. Thank You ... for forgiving me ... so I can now ... forgive myself. I love You. I feel ... Your peace. Thank You, Jesus. Amen."

Eugene was the first to hug her. Ken, Lydia Grace, Loretta, and Gloria were next; all of them crying. Carrie Emeline, Christopher, and Jerilyn rounded out the group.

"God bless you," said Christopher.

"God bless you, my sister in Christ," said Gloria.

"I have one last verse to read you," said Eugene with a noticeable catch in his voice. "This is from Second Corinthians chapter five and verse seven. 'Therefore if any man **be** in Christ, **he is** a new creature: old things are passed away; behold, all things are become new.' That's you now, Cecilia. How do you feel?"

Cecilia smiled. "Saved, forgiven ... and redeemed."

"Ahem," said Dr. Beasley as he cleared his throat and reentered the room. "Cecilia, Nurse Wilson is going to check your vitals."

They all stepped back so the nurse could do her job.

Within a few moments, Dr. Beasley said, "Cecilia, your vitals are regular, and I see no reason to keep you. I do want you to have counseling. In fact, I would like Gloria and Loretta to have counseling, also," he said as he looked toward the other girls. "You have all been through a very emotional time, for similar, but different reasons."

"Would you release Cecilia into Jerilyn's and my care?" asked Christopher. "She can stay at our home while she recovers – if that's okay with Cecilia, that is."

"It's okay ... with me. Thank you ... both ... very

much."

Dr. Beasley smiled. "I think that's a perfect solution. You'll only be two blocks away from me, so don't hesitate to call if you need me. Christopher, I'll loan you a wheelchair to take Cecilia to your home. Now, if you ladies will help Cecilia dress, Nurse Wilson can get this room ready for other patients." He looked at Cecilia and smiled. "I wish you all the best, young lady. God bless you."

"Thank you ... Dr. Beasley, for everything. God bless ... you, too."

Chapter Twenty-Three

The Reunion

*"Wait on the Lord: be of good courage,
and he shall strengthen thine heart: wait,
I say, on the Lord."*
Psalms 27:14

Sunday morning, December 24, 1967
Christopher and Jerilyn invited Gloria, Loretta, and Eugene to have breakfast with them at their home on South College Street on Christmas Eve. Cecilia was already there, settled in their guest room. Eugene had moved her out of Christmas Hotel, and a young couple had already reserved her room. Cecilia was recovering fine, and the hoarseness in her voice was nearly gone.

Lily, John, their four children, along with John's parents, had returned from Russellville, so Christopher and Jerilyn again had a full house.

Jerilyn threw her arms open wide as each new guest entered her home. "Welcome – and the more the merrier! We can make pallets on the floor for the children if necessary."

Following breakfast, Lydia Grace opened her presents. She said she couldn't wait to do it until after the noon meal at Christmas Hotel. From Christopher and Jerilyn she received a University of Cincinnati Bearcat jacket.

"Go ahead and support your UC Bearcats," said Ken. "Just remember, UC can't beat the University of Kentucky Wildcats in basketball."

"Maybe not in basketball, but what about football, big brother?" Lydia Grace quipped with a smug smile.

"Okay, you *may* have me there, but don't be *too* confident!" he said good-naturedly.

The rest of the friends and family laughed and shook their heads at their camaraderie.

When Lydia Grace opened her gift from Ken, it was a UC Bearcat football and signed by the current season team players. She punched his arm. "Thanks, big brother."

"Don't mention it, little sis," and he winked at her.

Cecilia enjoyed the interaction between the two. "You know, I'm really missing my two brothers. We all play like you two."

Lydia Grace put her arm around Cecilia. "I think you'll want to see them soon."

"Yes, you're right, I think I will."

From Lily and John, Lydia Grace received a book of the greatest piano compositions in the past four centuries. "Thanks, guys," she said as she hugged her oldest sister and brother-in-law. To John she added, "Have I ever told you that you're my favorite brother-in-law?"

John considered what she said and smiled. "Yeah, right. I'm your *only* brother-in-law," and everyone laughed.

Carrie Emeline presented her with an artist's painting of the fountain in Bowling Green, Kentucky. "Thank you, Carrie Emeline."

"You're welcome, Lydia Grace. You know, because I live and work in Bowling Green, I see the fountain daily, and I can never pass by the fountain without thinking of you. A sidewalk artist painted the fountain last summer. I couldn't resist buying it for you."

"I've got a present for you, too, Lydia Grace," said Chris.

Lydia Grace ruffled his hair. When she opened it, it was a framed photograph of her dog. "Aw, it's *Gabe*!"

Gabe thought he was being called and left the warm hearth, walked to her, and licked her cheek.

"Thanks, Chris. I miss Gabe when I'm away at school." She set the photograph on her lap and hugged the large German Shepherd with one arm, and Chris with the other. "Did you take the photograph?"

"Yes. Dad gave me a camera for my birthday in September."

"Well, you're a chip off the old block. Your photograph is every bit as good as any of Dad's."

"Thanks, Sis."

"Time for church," announced Christopher.

The family and friends walked the short distance from 210 South College Street to Christmas Hotel. Eugene had wanted to wheel Cecilia in the borrowed wheelchair from the clinic, but she said she'd be fine, as long as he held on to her.

He looked down at her and smiled. "Not a problem."

The service in the Christmas Hotel chapel was to begin at 10:30, and many of the regular congregation for the annual Christmas Eve service had arrived, along with the hotel guests. Lydia Grace sat at the organ and played the Christmas hymns. They left the doors open so that Mr. Mullins would be able to hear the service from his front desk, along with any spillover of people in the lobby.

Cecilia and Eugene sat together, next to Loretta and Ken. Gloria sat with Carrie Emeline, while Lily and her family and in-laws sat with Jerilyn. The congregation rose and sang the hymns that Lydia Grace played. Christopher stood in front of his chair behind the pulpit and sang with the congregation.

When the last hymn was sung, Christopher walked to his place in the pulpit. "Please remain standing, as we ask the Lord's blessing on this service. Dear Heavenly Father, we thank Thee that we could be here today to worship Thee and to thank Thee for the gift of Thy Son nearly two-thousand years ago. We realize that Thy Son Jesus is the reason for the Christmas season, and we thank Thee for sending Thy Son Jesus to join mankind, and become our Savior and Redeemer. Bless this service as we read part of the Christmas Story. In the name of Jesus we pray ... amen. You may be seated.

"As all of you regulars of our Christmas services know, we normally have the candlelight service in the evening on Christmas Eve and read the Christmas Story from the Book of Luke. Then on Christmas morning we read the Christmas Story from the Book of Matthew. This has been a tradition for many years at Christmas Hotel. I wasn't sure how to handle it this year, because Christmas Eve falls today on Sunday.

"Late last night my dilemma was solved when I received a phone call that has changed some of the procedure this Christmas. This morning, I will be reading from the Book of Luke. Tonight will be a very special Candlelight Christmas Eve service, so I hope you will all return. Tonight's service will begin at seven o'clock. Tomorrow morning on Christmas Day, the service will begin at ten-thirty, and I will read the Christmas Story from the Book of Matthew. With that said, please turn in your Bibles to the Book of Luke, and I will read from chapter two, verses one through twenty."

*****

Following the service, the family and friends gathered in the dining room for one of two special meals prepared by the Christmas Hotel chefs. Five tables joined together were needed to accommodate the group of family and friends. Many of the congregation headed to the dining room for the Christmas Eve noon meal. Today the chefs prepared a Waldorf salad, roast goose topped with a Cumberland sauce containing a combination of red currant jelly, orange and lemon zests, mustard and seasonings, along with side dishes of asparagus casserole, sweet potato casserole, oyster dressing, cornbread, and for desert, tapioca pudding or mincemeat pie.

The waiters asked all the guests to return for the Christmas meal the next day. "The Christmas meal will be just as special," they promised.

Following the huge meal, Ken asked Loretta, Gloria, Cecilia, Eugene, Lydia Grace, Chris, and Carrie Emeline to go for a walk with him. He needed to draw them away from the house, following his father's instructions.

"Where are we going?" asked Loretta.

"You'll see shortly." He looked back at Cecilia and Eugene who were bringing up the rear. "Cecilia, are you going to be okay for a walk of about six blocks or so? Or do you want me to get the wheelchair?" asked Ken.

"I'm fine, as long as I can hang onto Eugene."

"I'll carry you if need be. You can't weigh over a hundred pounds dripping wet. I know, because I carried you from Christmas Hotel to Dr. Beasley's office."

"So that's how I got there. I wondered about that. However, you should know, I weigh a hundred and fifteen pounds."

They entered Greenlawn Cemetery. "We're going to a cemetery?" asked Gloria, with a strange expression.

"Yes, but it's not just any cemetery. It has a lot of family history. Just follow me and I'll explain."

He stopped at a tall obelisk monument first. "Thomas Hoy and Lucy Goodnight Hoy. A prominent couple in Franklin in the nineteenth century," said Ken. "For you that don't know,

Thomas and Lucy Hoy built Christmas Hotel, and it opened in eighteen fifty. Their desire was for the miracle of Christ's birth to be celebrated daily. Thus the name and the year-around Christmas decorations."

From there he walked to the next two graves. On them Lydia Grace read aloud from the monuments:

Captain Jacob Barnabas Bazell
June 15, 1841 - May 29, 1942
God-fearing Man, Husband, Father, and Friend

Mary Eve Winters Bazell
August 1, 1843 - May 29, 1942
God-fearing Woman, Wife, Mother, and Friend

"Wow, they died on the same day," said Loretta.

"Yes," said Ken. "It was said at their funeral that the Lord couldn't separate them in death. They were that much in love, even at a century old." He stared at Loretta when he said it, and to his delight she blushed when he winked at her.

"Captain and Mrs. Bazell purchased Christmas Hotel from Mr. and Mrs. Hoy in eighteen eighty-three," continued Ken. "They sustained the mission of the Hoy family. The Bazells were an amazing Christian couple. They befriended my mother when she arrived here in December of nineteen forty-one, after receiving the news her husband had died at Pearl Harbor.

"Our mother went through a period of extreme depression. She was not only widowed, but had no money when she arrived in Franklin, Kentucky. She was twenty at the time – around the ages of you four girls." He paused a moment and pointedly looked at Cecilia, then Gloria, Loretta, and finally Lydia Grace. "She was also pregnant, and *very* scared."

The next grave they came to was the grave of Carrie Emeline Bazell. "My twin was named for her, and as you can see she died in eighteen eighty-four, soon after her parents bought Christmas Hotel. When Carrie Emeline Bazell was twenty years old, her fiancé died in a railroad accident. Her parents worried about her depression. She turned her back on God. After moving to Christmas Hotel, her heart began to heal. She asked God to forgive her. She rededicated her life to Him.

"When we were born," he said, pointing to his twin and himself, "I was named Kenneth Elliott Wright. Kenneth was for my biological father and Elliott, the masculine of Ellie, for Dad's first wife, and Lily's biological mother. Mom wanted my sister named for Carrie Emeline, the daughter of her benefactors, Mr. and Mrs. Bazell."

By now, Cecilia, Gloria, and Loretta were using tissues to dab at tears trailing on their cheeks.

Ken read the name on the next grave visited. "Eleanor Simmons Wright. So now you know where Lily's mom is buried. Lily named her youngest baby Ellie after her biological mama who gave *her* life. These next two graves are Dad's parents. They died in a car crash when Dad was just seventeen. They had gone on a second honeymoon trip down in Tennessee. A car hit them on the way back home, and they were both killed instantly."

"Oh, how awful," said Cecilia.

"As you know, my parents died in a car crash, too," Loretta said almost in a whisper. "I'm feeling differently about their deaths. My parents loved each other so much. I couldn't imagine one of them dying before the other. Maybe it's a blessing when they both died together, just like the Bazells and your grandparents."

"God knows what's best," said Ken. "As my mom says, if something tragic happens in our lives, God always has a plan B. Bad things *can* happen to good people, but we need to be faithful and trust God. Mom and Dad always say that no matter how painful a situation is when going through it, just trust in the Lord Jesus, and He will see you through. We can't control the evil in the world," Ken said, and hugged Loretta to his side.

There was silence while they beheld the rows of graves, then Ken continued. "My parents have told us many times to keep a diary, or write dates of things that happen to us in our Bibles when we do our morning devotions. We've all been surprised when we look at notes years later, of how God answered our prayers. It's not always the way we hoped at the time, but it's always answered in the best way. That's the way of our Lord Jesus. God loves you and He can help you through any situation. I think that everyone of us can now attest to that."

They all nodded in agreement.

"Well, that's what I wanted to show you. I wanted you to know that many before you have been through all sorts of tragedies, but God saw them through. Now we just need to look to Him for our future and trust Him in whatever happens." With that said, Ken turned to lead the others home.

They walked together quietly, stepping around the graves. As they neared the street, Gloria spotted a soldier in his United States Army dress uniform, watching them from the street curb. He was too far away for her to make out his facial features, but she knew that build and posture. Her heart rate quickened and Gloria picked up her pace, moving to the front of the group.

Reality dawned as she drew closer, and Gloria could no longer contain herself. She screamed and then cried out, *"It can't be! It can't be! Oh, it is!"* She took off in a sprint toward the man, and he ran to her. "Matthew, oh Matthew! I can't believe it's really you." The tears were streaming down her face. *"Matthew! Oh, Matthew!"*

They reached each other, and he removed his hat. She jumped into his arms and he caught her, twirling her around. "Gloria, my darling." He began kissing her all over her face, drew her close and kissed her on the mouth, and Gloria did not care who might be watching. When at last he released her, he set her down and held her at arms-length.

He gazed into her teary amber eyes, as she gazed back into his dark brown eyes. Now tears were trailing from his eyes, too. "I love you," he said. "I've missed you." His mouth trembled as he spoke the words.

"Oh, Matthew, I love you, and I've missed you so much!"

He kissed her again, hugging her close.

Matthew placed his hat under his arm and took her hands. He knelt on one knee. "I'm going to do this right this time. I've already asked your father if I can marry his daughter. This time it will be legal. Gloria, will you do me the honor of becoming my wife? I promise to love and cherish you all the days of my life."

"Yes, Matthew, oh, *yes!*"

He stood, placed his hands on her face, cupping her tear-streaked cheeks, and kissing her again.

When he finally released her, she blurted, "Matthew, we're going to have a baby."

"Your parents told me that, too, and I couldn't be happier."

She sighed in relief and leaned against him. "I'm so glad. I need to hear all about what happened to you."

Gloria turned around when her friends applauded and began to whoop and holler. She had forgotten all about them. She laughed. "I've got some new friends for you to meet, Matthew."

Her friends walked up to the happy couple, and she introduced them one by one as he shook their hands. Then Gloria laid her head on his shoulder, and they held hands and walked back to 210 South College Street.

Chapter Twenty-Four

The Mission

*"I waited patiently for the Lord; and he
inclined unto me, and heard my cry.
He brought me up also out of an horrible pit,
out of the miry clay, and set my feet upon a
rock, and established my goings.
And he hath put a new song in my mouth,
even praise unto our God: many shall see it,
and fear, and shall trust in the Lord."*
Psalms 40:1-3

Sunday afternoon, December 24, 1967
On the walk home, Gloria questioned Ken. "Did you know about this? Is that why you took us to the cemetery?"

"In answer to your questions, yes and yes. My dad received the call from your dad last night to say Matthew had been returned home from the Department of the Army. They all planned to drive down here this morning. *All*, meaning Matthew's parents, too. Dad wanted me to distract you until they arrived. The only part I didn't know was that

Matthew would show up at the cemetery."

"I couldn't wait to see Gloria," said Matthew. "I was given the directions and ran here."

"I chose the cemetery, thinking it would be a good place for distraction and a tour," said Ken. "I wanted you and the others to meet the people who had been here before, and the trials they went through. I wanted Gloria, Cecilia, and Loretta to realize that all of you need to put God first, and then everything would fall into place in due time. It may not always be what you hoped. In your case, Gloria, I think you got exactly what you wanted. I hope you'll not forget to put God first, just because Matthew is back."

"Don't worry, Ken, I won't fall into that trap again. When something awful happens, and it probably will, I'll trust God. I'm no longer the spoiled little girl I was before I arrived at Christmas Hotel. I hope and pray I've learned a lot."

*****

When the siblings and friends returned to the house, they were greeted by Gloria's parents Ralph and Irene Reynolds, and Matthew's parents Pastor Warren and Bertha Johnson. The group gathered in the living room. Christopher and Ken brought in extra chairs from the kitchen.

When they were all seated, Pastor Warren was the first to speak. "Matthew, your mother and

Gloria's parents know what happened to you, but I'm certain that the story is foremost on Gloria's mind. Are you ready to tell her?"

"Yes, sir, I am." He stared into Gloria's eyes and took her hand.

"My parents told me about being visited by two army officers on December eighth, approximately five weeks after my helicopter was shot down. It was a top secret mission, and the United States Army couldn't notify you about me being reported MIA until they'd exhausted every means of finding me. They finally believed that I was most likely dead. The army didn't want you and my parents to worry any longer because of my lack of contact.

"I still can't discuss the mission, as it's in progress to begin again with a new crew. However, I can tell you what I remember just before and much later after the chopper went down. The pilot did a splendid job of bringing us down in a controlled crash into a small forest of teak, palms, mangroves, bamboos, and tall grasses. It was a heavy landing. I must have been thrown a greater distance from my buddies. If I'd been seen, I would have been rescued by the others. I was later informed the rescue chopper arrived almost immediately, but was under heavy fire from the enemy on the ground. The crew couldn't see me and assumed I'd been captured. They had to get out fast.

"I must have been unconscious for a long time. The enemy evidently moved on, thinking the rescue was complete. Thankfully, they didn't find me. I remember when I awakened, I checked my watch, but it was broken. Obviously, I hit my head when I landed. I had lost some of my short-term memory and couldn't remember the mission, but I did know I was an American soldier, somewhere in Vietnam. I knew I was in pain and my head hurt. When I moved, I realized my chest and shoulder hurt, too. I remember thinking I had broken ribs.

"When I stood, my legs were okay, but my shoulder was dislocated. I lifted myself off the ground using one arm. My ankle was weak. I didn't think I sprained or broke it, but I probably pulled a ligament. It was getting dark, so I retrieved matches from my backpack to start a small fire. I had plenty of dead wood and brush to use. By this time, my memory was returning, and I realized that lighting a fire in enemy territory would be crazy.

"My shoulder, head, and chest throbbed. I don't know what hurt worse. I tried to knock my shoulder back in place, but it was too painful. I used my waterproof jacket for a tent covering and spread it in low hanging branches. In my back pack, I used a blanket in which to wrap myself and ate some beef jerky. As the darkness set in I fell into a restless sleep.

"I awakened just as the sun peaked over the horizon. I still couldn't remember much about the mission. I assumed I must have been in a plane or helicopter, because of my clothing. I didn't know how many were with me, and if they were dead or alive. I had a compass, but I wasn't sure about my location, beyond thinking I must be behind enemy lines, so I had no idea in what direction I should walk or how far to the base. I couldn't hear any sound of rescue or of my buddies searching for me. I thought they were either dead or captured. The pain was getting to me, and I sat down, so I wouldn't fall. I saw a Vietnamese man and a teenage boy walking toward me. Then I passed out."

The look of anguish on Gloria's face was obvious. Matthew patted her hand. "It gets better, honey. Remember I'm here now. Well, God must have sent His angels. I woke up in a grass hut. I looked around and a woman was sitting near me, sewing. I checked my shoulder and it was no longer dislocated. My chest was bandaged, but not too tight, and I was propped on a cot, I suppose to prevent pneumonia. The woman must have given me some type of pain reliever, because the pain was bearable, at least until I coughed. Then the pain intensified.

"The woman looked at me and smiled when she saw I was awake. She pulled on my dog tags around my neck and found my cross. She pointed at my cross, reached in the top of her dress, and showed me the cross on a chain around her neck. I thought, Here I am, somewhere in the enemy territory of Vietnam, and I encounter a Christian family. I couldn't believe it! That certainly wasn't luck. It was a miracle from God.

"She ran outside and called to someone. The man and teenager I saw before I fainted walked into the hut. The man smiled, and pointed at my ribs and shoulder, and then he pointed at his ribs and shoulder. I got the message. He had doctored my ribs and shoulder. His wife brought me what looked like a tea with roots floating in it. I drank it, and the pain all but went away, along with the cough. I don't know what roots were in the tea, but they certainly worked, and I was thankful.

"I must have stayed with them at least six weeks. I know my ribs had healed, and my memory returned." He turned and looked into Gloria's eyes. "Gloria, I thought about you many times during this ordeal. I knew you and my parents must be worried." He squeezed her hand and kissed her.

"I am just so sorry you had to go through this, Matthew. Yes, we were all worried, but I grew up during the process. I hope it never happens again, though!"

He smiled at her, brushed the hair from her face, and continued. "To conclude the story, the family and I learned each other's names, and when the father brought a friend, I also learned the English meaning of their names. The friend spoke broken, but understandable English. The friend's name was Hien, meaning gentle or quiet. The father was Bao, meaning protection, and the son was Binh, meaning peace. The wife and mother who nursed me was Mai, meaning golden flower. Hien handed me a piece of paper and a pen. He said the enemy soldiers had left the area, and he told me to write down the location of my base, and he could take me there.

"I hugged and thanked my benefactors before I left. Hien translated my words of thanks and appreciation to the Vietnamese family. I must say, being with this family was an amazing experience. I'd really like to know what was in that tea!" Matthew laughed along with the others in the room.

"It took seven days walking through the jungle to get to my base. The doctors checked me over and said I was in surprisingly good health. They chuckled and said the rice diet and the tea roots certainly hadn't hurt me any. They pronounced my ribs sufficiently healed, and boarded me on a plane to Hawaii the next morning.

"When I arrived at the United States Army-Hawaii base, I knelt and kissed the ground. I was on the next flight to Oakland Army Base, and then I arrived back in Gary, Indiana yesterday. I wanted to jump in the car and drive here immediately. My parents and your parents convinced me to wait until this morning to drive in with them and surprise you. They didn't want us arriving in the middle of the night, and they hoped to allow Mr. Wright time to procure a marriage license for a wedding. That is, if you said yes."

Gloria laughed. "Was there any doubt?" Then she kissed him. Pulling away, she frowned, "I don't have a dress to wear. I want to look pretty for you."

"You always look pretty to me," said Matthew, and he kissed her again.

"Yes, you do have a dress, dear," said Gloria's mom. "I brought my wedding dress, and I'd be honored if you'd wear it. I also brought white heels from your closet."

"Oh, Mom, thank you."

"Since I arrived late yesterday in Gary, and today's Sunday, and all the stores are closed, I wasn't able to buy you an engagement ring and a wedding band," Matthew said.

"Well, of course I don't have a wedding band for you either, Matthew."

"Again, our parents solved that problem, too," said Matthew, suddenly smiling.

Warren and Bertha Johnson rose and stepped forward. "This wedding band, and diamond and pearl ring, belonged to my grandmother; Matthew's maternal great-grandmother," said Mrs. Johnson. "We would be honored if you would accept them as our wedding gift to you both."

"Thank you, Mrs. Johnson. What a lovely gift." Gloria stood and hugged Matthew's mother. "I suppose I can now call you Mom."

"Yes, Gloria, you can." The two women hugged again.

Matthew's mother handed him the rings, and he placed the diamond and pearl engagement ring on Gloria's ring finger of her left hand, and again, he kissed her.

"Well, we have our gift, too," said Gloria's dad. "We have a man's wedding band you can give to Matthew. It was my paternal grandfather's. It's a little worn, but we polished it last night." He handed it to Gloria.

"Thank you, Mr. Reynolds ... Dad," said Matthew. "I'd be pleased to have Gloria place your grandfather's ring on my finger."

Jerilyn spoke next. "Gloria, you have a borrowed dress, old rings, now you just need something new and something blue."

Loretta smiled eagerly. "I have a blue lace-trimmed handkerchief you can carry. It belonged to my mother, and I brought it with me. I would be honored if you'd borrow it."

"That's perfect," said Gloria. "It's not only blue, but it will be a second borrowed item." She hugged Loretta and thanked her.

"I have something to cover the new," said Cecilia. "The day after I arrived, I explored around the square and stopped in Frank Shannon Jeweler on West Kentucky Avenue. They had a beautiful gold chain ankle bracelet I purchased. I haven't even worn it, but I'd be pleased for you to wear it."

Gloria stood and hugged Cecilia. "Thank you so much. I'd be happy to wear your ankle bracelet."

At that moment the doorbell rang. Judge Joe Moss James was welcomed into their home. "I have the marriage license," he announced, holding it up and waving it in the air.

"Thank you, Joe Moss," said Christopher. "It was nice of you to acquire this on short notice, *and* on a Sunday."

The judge laughed. "Just don't forget me at the next election!"

"Joe Moss, I hope you and your wife Jerri can join us at seven o'clock tonight in the chapel at Christmas Hotel for the wedding," said Christopher.

"Jerri and I wouldn't miss it. She always enjoys a wedding."

"Now, let's get these documents signed, so this marriage will be legal," said Judge James.

As soon as the proper signatures were on the license, the doorbell rang and in walked Pastor Palmer and his wife Mary. "We heard there was to be a wedding tonight. Mary and I didn't want to miss the wedding of the young woman who rededicated her life to Jesus in our church."

Christopher addressed Gloria. "Well, Gloria, you now have three pastors in attendance: Matthew's dad, Pastor Palmer, and me. You also have Judge James. You need to choose who will marry you two. I certainly won't be offended if you would prefer one of the others."

"May I talk it over with Matthew first?"

"You go right ahead, Gloria. Jerilyn and I are going to go ahead and finish decorating the chapel at Christmas Hotel. It will still be a candlelight service for your Christmas Eve wedding."

"Thank you, Mr. Wright. I'm sure I speak for Matthew, too that we appreciate everything all of you have done for us."

"You both are quite welcome," replied Christopher, patting her hand.

The doorbell rang again, and it was Carol Ann and James. Christopher welcomed them. Carol Ann viewed the crowd. "Oh, we don't want to intrude," she said. "We brought a thank you gift for Jerilyn, and then we'll go."

Jerilyn stepped forward. "You two are *not* intruding, and you're certainly *not* leaving just yet. Please come in."

"It's only some peach preserves I canned, and some bread I baked this morning. I just wanted to thank you for staying with me the night when James was out of town."

"Well, I thank you for the gift."

"It's going to be okay, Jerilyn," said Carol Ann. "James and I have decided to adopt. We *will* have that baby ... or older child. It just may take a few years on a waiting list."

"I'm happy about your decision," said Jerilyn. "There are many children needing homes."

"I'll corroborate that," said Eugene.

Cecilia walked up to Carol Ann. "I met you in the diner at the bus station when I first arrived in Franklin. You gave me directions to Christmas Hotel."

"I remember," said Carol Ann. "It's nice to see you again. This is my husband James," and the two shook hands.

Gloria also came forward with Matthew at her side, "I'm getting married tonight, and since we're both friends of the Wrights, and if you have no other plans, please come to our wedding in the chapel at Christmas Hotel."

Carol Ann looked at James, and he nodded. "We'd be delighted. What time?"

"Seven o'clock," said Gloria.

"Gloria, you can get dressed in our family's private room, which is room number seven," said Jerilyn. "It's a little larger than your room, and it will accommodate all the ladies who will help you dress. That's also the room I dressed in just before I married Christopher."

Jerilyn turned to Matthew. "Matthew, you can shower and get dressed in the men's dressing room behind the altar, which is used for the groom and those getting baptized."

"We'd all better get a move on," said Christopher. "I'm sure Gloria and Matthew don't want to be late for their own wedding!"

Chapter Twenty-Five

The Wedding

"Wherefore they are no more twain, but one flesh. What therefore God hath joined together, let not man put asunder."
Matthew 19:6

Sunday Evening, December 24, 1967
Gloria and Matthew chose Christopher to perform the wedding. They wanted to be married by an ordained minister, but they also desired for Matthew's father to be seated with Matthew's mom for the entire ceremony, except when he walked Gloria down the aisle. They also reasoned that it was at Christmas Hotel where Gloria began to heal, and Christopher was the pastor for the little chapel in Christmas Hotel.

Matthew had finished showering, and he was again wearing his army dress uniform. He was currently in the room behind the altar along with his two best men. He couldn't narrow it down to one, so Eugene and Ken would stand beside him. Gloria had the same dilemma. She wanted both

Cecilia and Loretta as her maids of honor. Chris would be the photographer.

In the beautiful chapel of Christmas Hotel, poinsettias decorated the altar, and white bows adorned the end of each of the pews. As the guests filed in, Lily's husband John handed each of them a candle while Lydia Grace played Christmas hymns on the church organ by candlelight. There would be no electric lights, not even in the lobby.

Gloria dressed in room #7 with the aid of her mother Irene, Bertha, Jerilyn, Carrie Emeline, Loretta, Cecilia, and Lily. They all helped her with the finishing touches. Carrie Emeline arranged Gloria's beautiful golden brown hair in a chic upsweep hairdo, adding a chain of pearls and poinsettia blooms. "She's breathtaking," said Cecilia, and the others concurred. Irene and Bertha began to cry.

"This is the second most wonderful day of my life," said Irene. She took the hand of her best friend, Bertha. "I never dreamed, when we married, that our children would fall in love and marry. Words can't express the happiness I'm feeling right now. I think our happiness can only be surpassed by Gloria and Matthew's."

"I agree, Irene," Bertha said, dabbing at her eyes.

Jerilyn nodded. "I understand completely. It

was in this very room on New Year's Eve, nineteen forty-one that my mother and my best friend prepared me for my wedding to Christopher. The questions my mother asked me were, 'What do you feel you have learned, and what has God taught you since you left home? What have you lost and gained?' How would you answer those questions, Gloria?"

Gloria pondered the questions before she answered. Looking straight into Jerilyn's eyes, she said, "I've learned to wait on God, and not jump to conclusions. I've lost my defiant and immature attitude, and I've gained hope in all situations. I've been reading the Bible, again." She pulled out the Bible in the nightstand and found the verses. "I stumbled upon Lamentations chapter three, verses twenty-four and twenty-five, which says, 'The Lord is my portion, saith my soul; therefore will I hope in him. The Lord is good unto them that wait for him, to the soul that seeketh him.'" She drew a deep breath and said, "I know that no matter what shall befall Matthew and me in the future, I pray that I will never become angry and rebellious with God again. I know He will see me through *any* situation."

Cecilia nodded. "I'd like to answer those questions, too. I've picked up the Bible again, too, and I began reading in the New Testament. When I read Matthew chapter twenty-three verse twenty-six, I memorized it. 'Thou blind Pharisee, cleanse first that which is within the cup and platter, that the outside of them may be clean also.' I was blind to Jesus Christ, even when He was always in my midst. I needed to clean the inside of my body, so that the outside would be clean. I needed to forgive myself, so Jesus Christ would show in me for all to see. I know I can go home now to Houston, because I *have* forgiven myself. Jesus cleaned me from the inside to the outside when He saved me, and I will forever be thankful. I've lost my rebellious attitude, too, and I've gained numerous wonderful friends."

Gloria, Loretta, and Carrie Emeline hugged her.

"I want to answer that, too," said Loretta. "I've been reading the Bible in *my* room, too. I started in the Psalms, and I've been learning what God says about the unborn." She asked Gloria to hand her the Bible, and Loretta quickly located the verses. "In Psalms one hundred and twenty-seven verse three, He says, 'Children are an inheritance of the Lord: and the fruit of the womb is his reward.' In Isaiah forty-four: verse twenty-four, He says, 'Thus saith the Lord, thy redeemer, and he that formed thee from the womb, I am the Lord that maketh all things.' I learned that God created all babies, no matter how they were conceived. He taught me that I can't play God and destroy His creation. I lost my naiveté, but I've gained the pleasure of giving. I'd like to give my baby to Carol Ann and James if they so desire. They want a baby so badly, and I need to move on with my life. I've prayed about this, and I feel content in this decision."

Jerilyn hugged her. "I know Carol Ann and James will be so happy for the gift of your baby, Loretta."

"Thank you, Jerilyn. Also, on January second, I'll return to Cincinnati with Lydia Grace. I'll tie up my parents' affairs and put the house up for sale. After that, I'll come back here to Franklin for the birth of my baby. I want Dr. Beasley to deliver the baby." She turned back to Jerilyn. "*And* I want you present, Jerilyn, so *you* can place the baby in Carol Ann's arms. After the baby is born, I'm going to transfer to UK to attend school for my final year of school."

Jerilyn again hugged her. "I think you have made two wonderful and unselfish decisions. Carol Ann and James will be wonderful parents. I also know that my son is going to be a very happy man knowing you're in Lexington."

By now, all the women were dabbing at their eyes from the testimonials of Cecilia, Gloria, and Loretta.

Lily brought out her gift to stop the tears. "I have a blue garter for you to wear, Gloria. Matthew will want to remove it later," and she winked at Gloria. It worked. The tears stopped and the women laughed.

Jerilyn's eyes sparkled when she addressed her oldest daughter. "Good gift, honey." She then said to the group of women, "However, we'd better get this wedding going. We can't have any more tears or we'll all need to redo our make-up!"

*****

Irene and Bertha descended the grand staircase to the chapel and joined their husbands. Lydia Grace still played hymns at the organ, and Lily and Carrie Emeline stood beside the organ, singing the Christmas songs. Gloria and Matthew had chosen four of their favorite songs to be sung by Lily, Lydia Grace, and Carrie Emeline, and one as background music while Christopher spoke to the congregation.

Jerilyn entered the chapel behind Carrie Emeline, and took a seat between Booker, Nettie Sue, and Robert McLemore on her one side, and Carol Ann and James on her other side. Jerilyn patted Carol Ann's hand and smiled. Christopher sat in his chair behind the podium, and three extra chairs were brought in for Matthew, Eugene, and Ken.

Lydia Grace played "Green, Green, Grass of Home," while she and her sisters sang. That was Christopher's cue to walk to his podium.

"I promised you something very special tonight. You have been given the honor of witnessing the wedding of Gloria Reynolds to Matthew Johnson, a United States Army soldier just home from Vietnam."

Matthew rose and walked to the podium and stood beside Christopher. Christopher shook Matthew's hand. "Thank you, Matthew, for your service."

The congregation stood and applauded. Matthew took his place beside the podium, and Eugene and Ken joined him. Earlier, Eugene and Ken did a coin toss of who would hand the wedding band to Matthew, and Eugene won.

Ralph Reynolds left his wife's side to join John and Chris at the chapel door. Chris had already snapped many pictures of the guests as they entered. Gloria and Matthew requested that "Never My Love" be sung next, and then "Your Precious Love" followed. That would be the cue for Cecilia and Loretta to descend the staircase and enter the chapel. They walked down the aisle, and they stood at the altar just opposite the two best men. Eugene stared and smiled at Cecilia, and Ken did the same with Loretta.

"Can't Take My Eyes off You" was sung next, and Gloria descended the staircase. Her father offered his arm at the door. She gazed down the aisle at Matthew. They only had eyes for each other, and a hush fell on the congregation. Lydia Grace then played the Wedding March, and the crowd stood in honor of Gloria. She made her way down the aisle and climbed the few steps up to Matthew.

Ralph Reynolds' eyes teared when he surrendered Gloria's hand to Matthew. He returned to the seat beside his wife. Ralph and Irene held hands and so did Warren and Bertha. All the other couples did the same. The betrothed stared into each other's eyes.

Christopher addressed the couple and his congregation. "I would like to read some verses from Ephesians chapter five. 'Submitting yourselves one to another in the fear of God. Wives, submit yourselves unto your own husbands, as unto the Lord. For the husband is the head of the wife, even as Christ is the head of the church: and he is the saviour of the body.

"'Husbands, love your wives, even as Christ also loved the church, and gave himself for it. For this cause shall a man leave his father and mother, and shall be joined unto his wife, and they two shall be one flesh.' Matthew and Gloria have written their own vows. Matthew, you may go first."

Matthew stared into Gloria's eyes. He cleared his throat and began. "I, Matthew, take you Gloria to be my wife, and my one true love in the presence of God and these witnesses. I will cherish our union, and I will love you more each day than I did the day before. I will trust you and respect you, laugh with you and cry with you, loving you faithfully through good times and bad, regardless of the obstacles we may face together. I give you my hand, my heart, and my love, from this day forward, for as long as we both shall live."

Eugene handed Matthew the wedding band, and he placed the band on her ring finger of her left hand. Gloria had returned the engagement ring earlier, and he retrieved it from his pocket and placed it behind the band.

Gloria gazed at him with such love that was obvious to all in attendance. She smiled at him and said, "I, Gloria, take you, Matthew, to be my friend, my lover, the father of my children and my husband, in the presence of God and these witnesses. I will be yours in times of plenty and in times of want, in times of sickness and in times of health, in times of joy, and in times of sorrow, in times of failure, and in times of triumph. I promise to love, cherish and respect you, to care and protect you, to comfort and encourage you, and dwell with you, for all our days on earth."

Loretta, who earlier won the coin toss with Cecilia, handed Gloria the gold band, and Gloria placed it on the ring finger of Matthew's left hand.

The ceremony returned to Christopher. "If anyone can show just cause why Matthew and Gloria should not be joined together, may you speak now or forever hold your peace."

The congregation remained silent.

"With the power vested in me, I now pronounce you man and wife. What God has joined together, let no man put asunder. Matthew, you may kiss your bride."

Matthew lifted Gloria's veil and kissed her with tenderness and love, then they turned to face the congregation.

"I give you Mr. and Mrs. Matthew Johnson," said Christopher.

The congregation stood. Matthew and Gloria walked down the steps of the altar and headed to the chapel's entry door. The cheers and the applause rang in the ears of the happy couple, along with the snapping of pictures from Chris.

Lydia Grace played the final requested song, Bobbie Vinton's "Please Love Me Forever." The guests set all the candles on a table just outside the door to the chapel. John snuffed out the candles and handed each wedding guest a bag of rice. The only light that lingered was that of the Christmas tree in the Christmas Hotel lobby.

As the happy couple climbed the staircase toward Gloria's room, family and friends threw rice at them for happiness and prosperity. When Gloria reached the top of the staircase, she turned around and tossed her bouquet.

Cecilia blushed when she caught it.

Chapter Twenty-Six

The Baptisms

"Trust in the Lord with all thine heart; and lean not unto thine own understanding. In all thy ways acknowledge him, and he shall direct thy paths."
Proverbs 3: 5-6

Christmas morning, December 25, 1967
Christopher and Jerilyn didn't have room for all the friends and family who were in town for breakfast at their home, so they invited them all to the dining room at Christmas Hotel. The entourage, which included John's parents and Cecilia, walked to the hotel. Eugene arrived in time to hold Cecilia's arm and steady her as she walked.

Matthew's and Gloria's parents now lodged at Christmas Hotel, Loretta still retained her room, and the newlyweds stayed in room #9. All of them, along with the group at the Wrights' home, met in the dining room. Christopher and Jerilyn called in advance for the dining room staff to pull at least ten tables together to accommodate everyone in their party.

Darius and Barbara Scott joined them, along with William. Eugene, who still held Cecilia's hand, guided her to the seat next to his, and Ken did the same with Loretta. Carol Ann and James had been invited, along with Judge Joe Moss, his wife Jerri, and their children. Lastly, Dr. and Mrs. Beasley and their children were invited to this special breakfast.

During breakfast, Matthew made a special request. "After the morning worship service, Gloria and I would like to be baptized by my father in the baptistery in the chapel. We want to begin our marriage completely renewed with a fresh start. Last night, I rededicated my life to the Lord, as Gloria told me she had done." He turned to his father. "Dad, would you re-baptize us today?"

"Yes, son, I think that's a fine decision. I would be happy to baptize you two ... again."

Loretta turned to Christopher. "Mr. Wright, would *you* please baptize me?"

"Me, too," echoed Cecilia. "I want to be baptized before another day goes by."

"That can be arranged," said Christopher, smiling. "I think the congregation would love to stay over for another happy event."

As soon as breakfast was finished, everyone found a seat in the little chapel. The congregation was huge again this Christmas morning, and once more spilled into the lobby.

Lydia Grace played Christmas hymns on the organ, while the congregation filed in. She then took her seat with Jerilyn, Carrie Emeline, and Chris. Lily sat with her husband, their children, and John's parents. Ken sat with Loretta, and Eugene sat with Cecilia. Gloria and Matthew sat with their parents.

Christopher stood, and the chapel quieted. "I'd like to read the Christmas Story from the Book of Matthew. Please turn into your Bibles to Matthew chapter one verses eighteen through twenty-five, and chapter two verses one through eleven."

When he finished reading, he said, "The Lord placed today's message on my heart. Years ago, I heard a sermon from another pastor about trust. Today, I would like to replicate what he preached, because I feel it's important for this service. My sermon is on the birth of Jesus, with the theme being trust.

"Mary had put her trust in the Lord. She was a virgin, who was only betrothed to Joseph. They were not yet married. Can you imagine how a young girl would be ostracized in that day? When a young woman has a baby without benefit of marriage, even in our year of nineteen sixty-seven, she can be treated brutally by others, no matter the situation. Mary had to place her trust in the Lord that everything would work out. In her day, she could have been stoned for adultery.

"Then there was Joseph's dilemma. He knew the people in town would think he had dishonored Mary, but he knew he hadn't. He had to both believe Mary's account of the angel, and believe the angel that visited him, that she was indeed with child by the Holy Spirit. Or he could make the choice to *not* believe the truth. Joseph had to place his trust in God.

"Then there are the people through all the generations from the day of Jesus' birth through the present. Are you going to place your trust for salvation and eternal life in the arms of Jesus? Will you trust Him to forgive you of your sins? Will you trust He is the Son of God and He has a plan for you?"

Christopher paused, and everyone in the chapel remained silent, gripped by his words. Then he said, "As we sing the invitational hymn, if you have not trusted the Lord to be *your* Savior, please come to the altar and we will take the Bible and show you how to receive the Lord's salvation through Jesus Christ. If you are a Christian, but you have fallen away from the Lord, and would like to rededicate your life to the Lord, please come forward and we'll pray with you. If you are saved and have not been baptized, I can baptize you today. So please come forward. As Lydia Grace comes to play "Just as I am," please stand and sing together as a congregation, unless you feel the need to come to the altar."

As the congregation began to sing, Matthew, Gloria, Loretta, and Cecilia stepped forward. Christopher smiled at them. When the congregation finished singing all five verses, Christopher asked the four young people to step up to the podium and face the audience.

"You will remember Matthew and Gloria if you attended their wedding last night here in the chapel."

Many in the congregation smiled and nodded.

"Actually, they both were saved and baptized many years ago, but they both recently rededicated their lives to the Lord, and have requested to be re-baptized to begin their marriage fresh. Loretta and Cecilia were saved since they came to Christmas Hotel. Jerilyn, please come and take the girls back to the ladies' dressing room to get ready."

Jerilyn came forward, at Christopher's request.

"Pastor Warren Johnson, will you please come forward?" To the congregation he said, "Pastor Johnson is the father of Matthew, and he will baptize Matthew and his new daughter-in-law Gloria. I will baptize Loretta and Cecilia. Pastor Johnson and Matthew, you can follow me to the men's dressing room to get ready. In the meantime,

Lydia Grace, please play some hymns, and you and Carrie Emeline can lead the congregation in song."

To the congregation he said, "You may all be seated," and he left the room with Matthew and Pastor Johnson.

The baptistery was located behind the pulpit. Normally, a wall with an empty cross, signifying the risen Christ was on the wall, but Ken and Chris stepped forward to slide back the wall to reveal the baptismal.

After the congregation sang all four verses of "Rock of Ages," and all four verses of "How great Thou Art," Christopher and Pastor Johnson appeared in the baptismal, one on each side.

Christopher asked Cecilia and Gloria to join him. They stepped down the four steps into the water and walked to Christopher. "I have three questions for each of you to answer. You may answer together.

"Do you now trust in Jesus Christ alone for the forgiveness of your sins and the fulfillment of all God's promises to you, even eternal life?"

"Yes," they both said loudly.

"Do you believe Jesus Christ died on the cross to pay your sin debt?"

"Yes," they said together.

"Do you intend with God's help to obey Jesus' teaching and follow Him as your Lord?"

"Yes," they responded together.

Christopher took Cecilia's hand and pulled her to him. He placed the handkerchief over her nose and mouth, and said, "On the profession of your faith in Jesus Christ as your Lord and Savior, and in obedience to His command, I now baptize you in the name of the Father, and of the Son, and of the Holy Spirit."

He submerged Cecilia in the baptistery, and she came up out of the water crying tears of joy.

Christopher next took Loretta's hand and pulled her to him. He placed the handkerchief over her nose and mouth, and repeated the same words to her. He immersed her in the water, and she came up out of the water crying and smiling.

Christopher looked to Pastor Johnson and nodded. Pastor Johnson asked his son and daughter-in-law the same three questions, and performed the same baptism of each of them as Christopher did for Cecilia and Gloria.

The congregation stood and applauded. Christopher asked Eugene to offer the closing prayer.

Chapter Twenty-Seven

The Gift of Life

"A gift is as a precious stone in the eyes of him that hath it: whithersoever it turneth, it prospereth."
Proverbs 17:8

Christmas late afternoon, December 25, 1967
After the baptism, Jerilyn asked Carol Ann and James to please come to Christmas Hotel around five o'clock, because someone had a gift to give them. "Afterwards, we'd like both of you to have dinner with us in the dining room at Christmas Hotel."

Carol Ann shook her head and smiled. "You don't have to give us a gift, Jerilyn. You've been more than kind to me, and I value your friendship."

"It's not from me," said Jerilyn. "I'm not at liberty to say. This person wants to tell you, and in person."

Carol Ann and James wore puzzled expressions on their faces, but they agreed to return to Christmas Hotel at five o'clock.

*****

Carol Ann and James arrived at five o'clock sharp. Chris was on duty at the front desk and asked them to head up the staircase to room #7. The door was already open when they arrived.

"Please come in and take a seat in the two brocade chairs in front of the window," said Jerilyn.

Christopher and Loretta joined them within minutes. Along with the desk chair, two more chairs had been added to accommodate the five of them.

"Loretta has something to say to you," said Jerilyn.

Loretta scooted her chair close to Carol Ann. She had rehearsed this speech last night. This was a big decision, and she wanted Carol Ann to know that she wanted to give her this gift of her baby out of love for Jerilyn and Jerilyn's friend. "I know you don't know me, but I know about you. I overheard you tell Jerilyn in Dr. Beasley's office that you were there for the results of tests. I again overheard you walking out of Dr. Beasley's office with Jerilyn. You were in tears. You said that it was your fault that you would never conceive, and that you had had three miscarriages. Please don't think that I was deliberately eavesdropping. I felt sorry for your situation. I wished you were pregnant and not me. When I went into the examination room, I was bitter and rude to Dr. Beasley. He did not mince words in letting me know that I was carrying a baby and not a *thing*. He was right.

"I was also at the Wrights' home when you brought the canned peach preserves and homemade bread. I know you desperately desire to have a baby, and you're unable to conceive. When you were at the Wrights' home, I heard you tell Jerilyn you've decided to adopt."

Both Carol Ann and James looked taken aback.

Loretta took a deep breath. "Please don't think I've been prying into your privacy, so please hear me out. First, I need to tell you a bit about myself, I'm a college student, and my parents recently died. I have a much older brother, but he's in the United States Air Force, and he's stationed in Germany. I'm unmarried, and I'm almost eleven weeks pregnant. My baby was not conceived in love." She paused and placed her hand on her stomach. "I have just recently been saved by the grace of God, but I know that at this time I would not be a good mother to my baby. Carol Ann, I know that you would be a wonderful mother." She sighed loudly, looked intently into Carol Ann's eyes, and then took her hand. "The reason I asked you here today on Christmas is to offer you the gift of my baby. He or she is due on July fourth. You are the couple I want to be the parents and raise my baby."

Carol Ann began to cry, looked toward James,

and he took her other hand and kissed it.

Through glistening eyes, James returned his gaze to Loretta. In a hoarse voice he said, "Please don't say this if you might change your mind. It would break Carol Ann's heart – and mine." Loretta turned toward James to look him square in the eyes. "Don't worry. I've given this much thought. I won't change my mind. I want you two to be the parents of this child. I'm leaving after the New Year to return to Cincinnati with Lydia Grace. I need to clean out my dorm room and finish settling my parents' estate in Cincinnati. When that's complete, I'll return to Franklin in plenty of time before the baby is born. I want Dr. Beasley to deliver this baby, with Jerilyn Wright and Carol Ann present. I want Jerilyn to place the baby in the arms of Carol Ann."

Carol Ann cried even harder, and jumped up to hug Loretta. Loretta stood and hugged her back.

"I don't know what to say, except thank you," said Carol Ann.

Christopher stepped into the corridor and made a motion with his hand. Judge Joe Moss James entered with some papers in his hand. "I have the papers for all involved to sign," the judge said. "This will make it official. Private adoptions are rare, but legal."

He handed the pen to Loretta, then to Carol

Ann, and finally to James for all to sign. Christopher and Jerilyn witnessed the document.

"My secretary will make up copies for both parties tomorrow morning. You may pick them up after noon. Congratulations, James and Carol Ann. You are a deserving couple." He shook both of their hands and left.

"I have something to give you," said Loretta. "This is a picture of what your baby looks like at around ten weeks." She produced the picture in her purse and handed it to Carol Ann, who cried anew.

"Thank you, Loretta. I never expected a gift such as this today ... on Christmas. This is the best Christmas gift I could have received. God bless you."

"God bless you, too, Carol Ann."

Chapter Twenty-Eight

Forgiveness and Hope

"Thou hast turned for me my mourning into dancing: thou hast put off my sackcloth, and girded me with gladness; To the end that my glory may sing praise to thee, and not be silent. O Lord my God, I will give thanks unto thee forever."
Psalms 30:11-12

Christmas Evening, December 25, 1967
After dinner at Christmas Hotel, Eugene walked Cecilia back to the Wrights' home, with her arm linked through his. "Would you like to attend the candlelight service at Christmas Hotel on New Year's Eve?" he asked along the way.

"I've planned on it." She stopped walking and looked up at him. "I also plan to leave for Houston the next day. I've already purchased my bus ticket." His countenance fell, and she realized he was crushed.

He swallowed and licked his lips before asking, "Will I ever see you again?"

"I've hoped to have the opportunity to discuss

something with you. I want you to know something very important, and now appears to be the appropriate time. You're aware I had an abortion. Two doctors have now explained the consequences of my poor decision. My abortion was performed in a dirty back-street old building; I can't even call it a clinic. However, I was informed that it was unlikely to make any difference even if the abortion had been performed in a sanitary hospital. Because of my age, my womb may be weakened enough that I may *never* be able to carry a baby to term."

Cecilia paused to gauge Eugene's reaction.

"Eugene, I don't want our relationship to progress any further without you knowing this. It hurts to know I may have destroyed my chances at having my own baby, and all because of one bad decision. I'm going to seek counseling when I return to Houston. I didn't understand all the ramifications, or I'd never have had the abortion. I believed the information I was given. I was told that it wasn't even a baby in the first trimester. I should have checked the facts more carefully. I also didn't realize the possible harm to my body. My boyfriend Ernie was a louse, but I could have carried the baby and given the baby up for adoption like Loretta is doing."

Eugene stopped her and turned her toward him. She looked down at the sidewalk, and he tipped her chin so he could look into her eyes. "Look at me, Cecilia."

She stared into his eyes and through her teary eyes, she saw the tenderness.

"Cecilia," he said earnestly, "please listen to me. I want you to know that I care deeply for you. The first fourteen years of my life, I was raised by two despicable human beings. If our relationship someday results in a marriage union, I would have no problem adopting children. In fact, even if you *can* carry children to term, I would still want to adopt, too. The Scotts adopted my three siblings and me. They had no intentions of breaking up our family. I would want to do the same for another family of children.

"I'm a teacher, so I'll never be rich. Therefore, if we do marry someday, I can't provide frills and luxuries for you. However, I'm a good steward of my dollars, so I can provide for you adequately, and any children we should be blessed to have naturally or through adoption. Most importantly, you and our children would know love."

Cecilia studied Eugene and bit her lip. "I'm not sure. I think you deserve better."

"Cecilia, don't put yourself down. Yes, you made a mistake, but that's not a problem for me. We've all made mistakes. Let's see where our relationship will go. The school term is over here on May twenty-ninth, the day before Memorial Day weekend. At that time, I can drive to see you, or you could come back here to Franklin. In the meantime, we can write lots of letters, and I can afford a long-distance call at least once a week. I want to get to know you better, Cecilia. I want to see if God wants us to marry." He paused and then said, "I hope I'm not going too fast."

"You're not going too fast, Eugene. I care about you, too, and I want the same as you." A tear slid down her cheek. Eugene wiped the tear for her. "What you have suggested is a good plan, Eugene. Now that God has forgiven me, and I have forgiven me, I need to see my parents. It's time."

"I know it is, Cecilia, but I'll miss you."

"I'll miss you too, Eugene."

He kissed her under the decorated street light, and she didn't care who saw them.

Chapter Twenty-Nine

The Prodigal Daughter Returns

"And he arose, and came to his father. But when he was yet a great way off, his father saw him, and had compassion, and ran, and fell on his neck, and kissed him."
Luke 15:20

January 03, 1968

It was a long ride on the bus. Cecilia had left Franklin two days earlier, and although she was anxious, she was also happy and excited to return to Houston. She had come full circle. She still had Mr. Woodson's phone number, and she called him from the bus station.

When he pulled up to the curb, he jumped out and hugged her. "It's good to see you, Cecilia!"

"It's wonderful to see you, too, Mr. Woodson." She smiled up at him.

"You look happy and at peace."

"I am. I have so much to tell you. I'm glad it's a long drive home."

He took her suitcase, and held the door for the

front seat. "This fare is on me, Cecilia."

She thanked him, and then began by saying, "Christmas Hotel was everything you and Mrs. Woodson said it would be. When I arrived in Franklin...."

*****

Cecilia finished her story just as Mr. Woodson turned the corner onto her street. It was a balmy sixty-eight degree day, and she could see her dad and her two brothers playing basketball in the driveway. The three of them stopped their game and stared as the taxi came to a halt.

"Goodbye, Mr. Woodson. I thank you and Mrs. Woodson for everything you did for me. I'll keep in touch. God bless you and your family."

"God bless you, too, Cecilia. God go with you." He patted her hand, and she kissed his cheek.

Cecilia opened the door and stepped out. Her father saw her and ran to the door of their home. He yelled to her mother, *"Doris, come quick! Cecilia's home!"*

He ran towards Cecilia, and she ran to him, the tears streaming down both of their faces. He hugged her to him and kissed her cheek. The prodigal daughter had come home.

Epilogue

*"In whom we have redemption through his
blood, the forgiveness of sins, according to
the riches of his grace;"*
Ephesians 1:7

Matthew and Gloria spend their army allotted two-
week honeymoon at Christmas Hotel before
Matthew is required to return to his new army base.
He is reassigned stateside at Fort Bragg, North
Carolina, for the remainder of his tour. Their son is
born on July ninth, and they name him Kenneth
Eugene Johnson. The following year, Gloria enrolls
in classes at Duke University in North Carolina. She
eventually fulfills her life-long dream of becoming a
nurse.

Cecilia, her parents, and brothers, arrive at
Christmas Hotel for Memorial Day weekend, 1968.
After the long distance romance with much prayer,
letters, and weekly phone calls, Cecilia and Eugene
realize they are in love and choose to marry.
Christopher performs the wedding on Saturday,
June first. Matthew and Gloria drive over for the
ceremony. Loretta is already in Franklin. A very
pregnant Gloria and Loretta are Cecilia's two maids

of honor. Ken arrives from Lexington, and he and Matthew are the two best men. Eugene and Cecilia choose to make their home in Franklin. In the course of three years, Cecilia has three miscarriages. Over the following five years, they adopt a family of two children, both boys, and a family of three children, two girls and a boy.

Loretta returns to Cincinnati with Lydia Grace on January 02, 1968. Loretta informs Lydia Grace that she is leaving UC, so she will no longer be her roommate, but she's sure God will send her someone else who is in trouble, and has need of the Lord. In February, after Loretta finally settles the affairs of her parents' estate, she heads to Lexington. She purchases a charming three bedroom home with Ken's blessing. The home is in a lovely old neighborhood and a short commute to UK, where she enrolls for the fall semester. With Ken's help, she is able to fix the minor disrepairs that made the exquisite turn-of-the-century home affordable.

In late May, two days before the wedding of Cecilia and Eugene, Loretta returns to Franklin and lives with Carol Ann and James until the baby is born. Carol Ann and James wish to better know the mother of their child. Loretta helps them ready the nursery, the room where Loretta sleeps in a twin bed. Right on time, on July fourth, Dr. Beasley delivers the seven pound four ounce baby girl in the home of Carol Ann and James. Jerilyn is in attendance as planned. Dr. Beasley hands the baby to Jerilyn. Jerilyn washes the baby girl in the Bathinette, and places her in the arms of Carol Ann. Later, Loretta laughs and says to Carol Ann and James, "You'll always remember her weight and birth date, since they are both the same, *and* on Independence Day!"

"I can't thank you enough for this wonderful gift," says the tearful Carol Ann. She glances toward James and he nods. "We've already agreed that if the baby is a girl, she should be named for both of her mamas. Her name is Lori Anna."

"Thank you. I appreciate that. I'll never forget you, Carol Ann."

"Nor I, you, Loretta."

On July ninth, Loretta returns to Lexington. She continues the relationship with Ken, and joins his church in Lexington. After her graduation from UK on June 11, 1969, they marry at Christmas Hotel. Cecilia and Gloria are Loretta's matrons of honor, and Matthew and Eugene are Ken's best men. The three couples become life-long friends.

The End

Smile, because your mother chose life for you.
If she's living, thank her.

*"Finally, brethren, farewell. Be perfect, be of
good comfort, be of one mind, live in peace; and
the God of love and peace shall be with you."*
2 Corinthians 13:11

*"Those things, which ye have both learned, and
received, and heard, and seen in me, do: and
the God of peace shall be with you."*
Philippians 4:9

*"For thou hast possessed my reins: thou hast
covered me in my mother's womb.
I will praise thee; for I am fearfully and
wonderfully made: marvelous are thy works;
and that my soul knoweth right well.
My substance was not hid from thee, when I
was made in secret, and curiously wrought in
the lowest parts of the earth.
Thine eyes did see my substance, yet being
unperfect; and in thy book all my members
were written, which in continuance were
fashioned, when as yet there was none of them."*
Psalm 139:13-16

Author's Notes:

Although all my books are works of fiction, I do like some real people to "visit" my stories.

Dr. L.F. Beasley was a practicing physician in Simpson County, Kentucky from 1934 until he retired in April, 1975. He served in WWII beginning sometime in 1942. He made house calls until he retired, delivered many babies, and conducted many surgeries. He died in 2011 at the age of 103. His mind was good; he drove his car until age 99, and played golf into his late 90s! He did not like his given names, therefore he went by his initials L.F., and so I will not reveal his given names either. (Information provided by his daughter Barbara Beasley Smith of Franklin, Kentucky)

Judge Joe Moss James was a paratrooper in the Korean War from 1952-1955. He was the Simpson County Sheriff from 1962-1966, and later a Simpson County Judge from 1966-1977. He married Geraldine (Jerri).
(Information provided by his daughter Jan Murphree)

Other "visitors" to the story were my husband Robert E. McLemore, his parents Nettie Sue Harris McLemore (currently resides in Bowling Green, KY) and James (Booker) E. McLemore (now deceased). Also, Mama Harris (deceased) who was Robert's grandmother. Jimmy McLemore my husband's brother is also deceased.

Christmas Hotel, the first book in the Christmas Hotel series was inspired by an article from January, 2008, in the Franklin Favorite, the newspaper in Franklin, KY. The article spoke about a diary left behind in the now razed Keystop Motel in Franklin, KY. The diary, dated 1873, possibly belonged to a young girl named C.E. Bazell from Rock Camp, Ohio. An Ohio assistant librarian traced the diary to a girl named Carrie E. Bazell who lived in Rock Camp with her parents until the late 1800s. Carrie Bazell died March 20, 1884 at the age of twenty-one, according to a brief obituary.

The inspiration for *Christmas Redemption* came to me while mowing the grass, of all places, back in June, 2013. It stemmed from an episode with a pro-life theme that I watched that week on "The Winning Walk" by Pastor Ed Young from the Second Baptist Church in Houston, Texas. The episode was titled "The Fetus is not a Baby."

As of this Writing:

Abortion/Adoption Hotline Information:
National Right to Life
Phone: 202-626-8800 Web site:
www.nrlc.org or

Focus on the Family:
Phone: 800-232-6459 Web Site:
www.focusonthefamily.com – or
email: help@focusonthefamily.com

National Adoption
Phone: 800-923-6602 Web site:
www.nationaladoptionhotline.org

Life Issues Institute
Phone: 513-729-3600
Email: info@lifeissues.org

Depression Hotline:
Crisis Call Center
Phone: 800-273-8255

Drug and Alcohol Hotline:
The National Alcohol and Substance Abuse
Phone: 800-784-6776

Suicide Prevention Hotline:
Phone: 630-482-9696

Abuse: Physical, Verbal, and Sexual Hotline:
Rape, Abuse Network
Phone: 800-656-4673

Anger Management Hotline:
Crisis Call Center: Phone: 800-273-8255

Christmas Redemption
Discussions and Questions for Book Club

1) What passages strike you as insightful, even profound? Is there a bit of dialogue that is funny or poignant that summarizes Cecilia, Gloria, and Loretta? Is there a particular comment by the three women that states the book's thematic concerns? Do you feel the three young women grew and matured by the end of the story?

2) Do the characters seem real or believable? Can you relate to their predicaments? To what extent do they remind you of yourself, or others, in the past or present?

3) Did certain parts of the book make you uncomfortable? Did this lead to a new understanding of awareness or an aspect of your life you had not thought of before?

4) What is the book's most important message? Why do you think the author wrote this book?

5) Discuss abuse and the loneliness, worthlessness, insecurity, anger, bitterness, abandonment, deceit, and other emotions felt by the three young women.

6) How did you feel emotionally regarding the opening chapter with Cecilia receiving the abortion? Did you have compassion or anger toward her after the abortion? Was she selfish? Or was she simply depressed and overcome by bitterness and unhappiness? If so, is that an acceptable excuse?

7) What are your thoughts about Gloria and Matthew performing their own wedding vows before God, without benefit of clergy? Keep in mind that the year is 1967.

8) What are your thoughts about the drugs and alcohol of which Cecilia and Loretta partook? Did you sympathize with them in any way?

9) Discuss the consequences of verbal, physical, and sexual abuse on a young woman.

10) How did you feel about Loretta attending the fraternity party so soon after burying her parents?

11) Is the plot engaging? Is this a plot-driven book:

a fast-paced page turner? OR did the story unfold too slowly with a focus on character development? Did you find the plot predictable? What did you think of the plot development? How credible did the author make it? Was the ending satisfying? If not, why and how would you change it?

12) How did you feel about Loretta's decision to have Carol Ann and James adopt her baby? Were you surprised? Pleased? Upset that she didn't keep the baby? Worried about the future relationship between Loretta, and Carol Ann and James, as the baby grew older?

A Sneak Peek of the Fourth Book in the Christmas Hotel Series: Christmas Pact. Enjoy!

Chapter One

At Christmas Hotel

"Hear me speedily, O Lord: my spirit faileth: hide not thy face from me, lest I be like unto them that go down into the pit. Cause me to hear thy loving kindness in the morning; for in thee do I trust: cause me to know the way wherein I should walk; for I lift up my soul unto thee."
Psalm 146: 7-8

The Present Day
Early Morning, Monday
December 02, 1974
Carrie Emeline lay on her back on the bed in Room #7 at Christmas Hotel and cried out in despair to God. "My life is a mess, and I'm only thirty-two. Dear God, I never thought my marriage would come to this. I never expected to be in this situation. I always thought I'd be married 'until death we do part'. I expected a fairy tale marriage ... like my parents' marriage ... like my siblings' marriages."

Sitting up, she grabbed a tissue on the

nightstand to wipe the tears that streamed down her cheeks and into her ears. Snatching another tissue, she blew her nose and threw the tissues into the overflowing waste basket with the others. *I've got to get myself together. My parents are worried. How can I possibly tell them about all the years since I married? I never let on to them that anything was amiss. I led them to believe the marriage wasn't perfect, but it was satisfactory. Anyway, they discovered it was far from perfect when Angela was born. I'm going to have to tell them I've been living a lie. How do I break the hearts of the two people I love so much?*

Rising from the bed, Carrie Emeline grabbed her robe, and quickly pulled it on, tossing her long, brown, wavy hair over the collar. While tying the robe, she crossed the room, opened the heavy drapes, and peered out the window. She unlocked the french doors and stepped out on the balcony, escaping the stuffy room. Gripping the railing, she looked down onto the square. Although the sun had not yet risen, she could tell from the streetlights that the square was decorated. She knew from past experience, the Christmas decorations had gone up the day following Thanksgiving. All the light poles in the square of the town's park-light setting had holly wrapped around them with a red bow at the top. Christmas wreaths adorned the doors of the businesses surrounding the square.

Not much about the town had changed in her lifetime. Some of the businesses had come and gone, along with the people of Franklin, but love from the townspeople prevailed. She sighed, looked down at the balcony, and looked back up. "Is there hope for me, Lord? Will I ever be happy again?"

She thought about the final divorce papers she had received at her Louisville home in early November. She knew the papers were coming, but actually holding them and reading the fact that divorce was inevitable caused her misery.

Was our marriage doomed from the start?

Down below, a bearded man sat on a bench inside the square and under a streetlight. He appeared to be elderly. She couldn't place him from the townspeople. He didn't look like the other men that congregated on the square, sometimes whittling or simply shooting the breeze. Wearing farmer's overalls, a heavy plaid shirt, and a large floppy hat, he sat feeding the pigeons and the doves. One of the doves took flight and landed on the railing around her balcony. The bird stared at her, and Carrie Emeline stared back. Human and bird locked gazes for about thirty seconds, and then the dove flew off. *That was strange.*

She glanced down toward the man in the park and found him looking up at her. He smiled and waved, and she returned the wave. *He appears to know me, or maybe he's just being friendly.* She tilted her head. *There's a familiarity about him.* Shivering, she stepped back inside, closed the french doors and the drapes. "Now what, Lord? How do I go about the business of living again?"

Checking her watch, she realized it was nearing six o'clock, time for the breakfast meal at Christmas Hotel. *I can't face people yet. I don't think I slept much last night. I'll drive to the truck stop and grab a light breakfast.*

In the bathroom she stared at her face in the mirror, and her red-rimmed blue eyes stared back at her. The bruising was finally gone, leaving only a few small scars from the cuts six months earlier. She ran warm water and washed her eyes and face. After brushing her teeth, she picked up the hairbrush to untangle the waves of her long hair. Her thoughts recalled the day she met Andrew, and she smiled for the first time in weeks.

Christmas Pact will be released October 11, 2019 and available for pre-order nearer that date.